Rev.

An eye and spirit opener. A must read for all young people of faith intending on entering college as well as their parents. An insightful story that dares to expose the religious intolerance of our nation; but yet is powerful enough to touch your heart. Highly recommended.

—*Rev. Dr. Walter L. Davis III*
City of Faith Tabernacle Church of God in Christ
Pastor and Founder

****

The Mis-education of Joy is a thought provoking work to be read through more than once, each time offering new instances of revelation and understanding. The author takes very sophisticated theological questions and simplifies them, making them assessable to the intellectual as well as those new to the faith. It is a true page turner that reminds us that faith persists not because we will it; but because it has a presence and force all of its own. The Mis-education of Joy is long overdue.

—*Gaelle Affiany,*
Graduate Student: Columbia University

****

Every parent's fear is put to rest by the redemption of the character of Joy. Her journey to find the deep roots of her faith ends when she realizes that answers to her questions weren't enough to give her purpose. Non Christians will be challenged and Christians will be encouraged to know that the Word of God is believable and trustworthy and will stand when critics use logic and reason to test your faith.

—*Myra Rosa*
Science Teacher: New York City

The *Mis*-Education of Joy

A Story by Paul C. Agard

First published by Dog Ear Publishing
4010 W. 86th Street, Ste H
Indianapolis, IN 46268
www.dogearpublishing.net

dog ear
PUBLISHING

ISBN: 978-160844-203-4

To
My sister Holly
A source of strength and encouragement.

To
My wife and children
My family
My prayer group
My friends
Thank you all for your ongoing support.

To
My editor Susanne Lakin
The need to inspire an author
is equally as important as perfecting his craft.
Thank you.

In loving Memory of
Winston Anthony Gooding

Introduction

"Congress shall make no law respecting an establishment of religion, *or prohibiting the free exercise thereof...*" *The First Amendment*

"The Bible is filled with fairytales" "Christianity is a vicious religion with a murderous past" "God does not exist" and "There is no evidence that a man named Jesus ever walked this earth." These are statements you would expect to hear at an atheist rally; but surprisingly, they are statements made in some American colleges, many of which receive federal funds. What is alarming is that these are not the words spoken by classmates during a discussion, but by instructors during a lesson. When it comes to religious rights in our nation, the question is, "Have we advanced or have we fallen away?" To determine this, we need to take a look back.

From 1776-1787, the founders of this country hammered out a revolutionary document based on the political ideologies of their scholarly predecessors and the greatest minds of their day. The framers drafted a social contract called *The Constitution* that categorized all aspects of their new society, from the separation of powers in government down to the right for their citizens to assemble. When it came to religion and how to approach it, the founding fathers drew heavily on men like John Locke, a 17th century English philosopher. They adopted his ideology that religion and belief was a natural right given to us by our creator. It is an inalienable right that must not be trampled. This union of the Constitutional law and the inalienable rights of religion gave birth to the First amendment. It was the framers firm position that no government institution can force you to believe against your conscience. Belief was your right.

As we fast forward to present day, we find our nation burying its religious heritage as it attempts to become more secular. In light of this, the First Amendment is continually reinterpreted and consequently, it is our inalienable rights that hang in the balance. Today, in many of our nation's colleges, Christian worldviews and traditional moral values are ridiculed and labeled outdated. Since my return to college in 2002, I have helped a number of students recover their faith. A faith lost as a result of professors who were insensitive to the beliefs of the students they taught. But there is one student whom I will always remember. A young girl whom I did not notice until it was too late. It is her story I wish to tell.

Joy Hunter is the name that I have given this girl who has etched out a permanent place in my heart. I never knew her neither was I aware of her struggle until the day she rejected her faith. I have asked myself repeatedly what I could have done to help her. My introspection has left me with one answer. I cannot help everyone especially if I am not aware of their plight. I can though be sensitive to the personal beliefs of others. This is a courtesy not limited to fellow students, but one that instructors must honor as well.

Within the pages of this book are *two* stories: the story of a young girl with a beautiful spirit, struggling to hold on to her faith, and the story of *my* struggle to tell her tale. The reader will encounter the arguments that challenged the young girl's core beliefs as well as the counterarguments. This will enable the reader to analyze the weaknesses and strengths of these arguments and equip themselves with the proper response. Inevitably, though, it is the love of God that jumps off the pages as Joy Hunter proves the beauty of the Christian faith is not found *just* in an argument, but in the life-changing power of God.

The book seeks to address three key points, 1. Many students enter into college unaware that the secular academic environment may be contrary to their beliefs, 2. Consequently, these students may find themselves Biblically ill-equipped and lacking the discussion skills needed to address the challenges to their faith. 3. Instructors need to be more sensitive to the beliefs of their students when dispensing the course material.

Just as with any other right granted to citizens, a student's religious beliefs should be respected in any institution that receives federal funds. When they are not respected, it is an infringement of the students First Amendment rights: *"The right to believe."*

Chapter One

The Revelation of the Vision

"Why don't you shut the @#%* up!"

Paul couldn't believe what was happening to him. He had been rendered helpless, unable to move. Usually he was quick with an intelligent comeback, but this time— nothing.

"You can damn well go to hell."

She was so close to him that Paul could smell her perfume and at the same time feel the very force of each profane word that she screamed at him.

"To hell with you! To hell with you!"

She's so beautiful. How can she say such ugly things? Paul thought.

"There are other people in this class too, you know," the young girl contended. "And you keep taking up the professor's time with your religious garbage."

Paul tried his best to speak. "I—I—" but no words would come out, and the beautiful young college student would not let up.

"I'm sick of this. I'm sick of you."

It was no use. He was paralyzed. Not just by the girl, but by all the other students in the class whose stares were just as loud as her words. Paul could almost feel their thoughts. Hatred, pity, contempt, and worst of all—shame.

Paul waited and prayed, that the professor would save him by bringing order to the class. But why would the professor help him? The professor was his enemy, an open atheist, his nemesis. In fact, the professor was the cause of Paul's current dilemma. He and Paul always argued during class and the beautiful girl, who had taken the professor's class before, was just showing her loyalty by coming to the professor's defense. But Paul still waited for help.

"You're a fanatic; that's what you are!"

But no help came. Paul was now gripped with doubt.

Maybe she's right. Maybe I am a fanatic, maybe I should shut up. These were the thoughts that raced through his mind. He whispered to himself, "Help me, God."

Just then, Paul felt someone grab his arm. It was Juan, his only friend in the class. Juan pulled Paul out of the room as the beautiful girl turned toward the crowd of students. But even from out in the hall, they could hear the laughter and snickering back in the class.

"It's okay, Paul," said Juan. "They're not rejecting you, they're rejecting God."

"Thanks, Juan," Paul replied. "But somehow I feel like they are rejecting me. I wanted to say something spiritual to that girl back there but the only thing I could think of was, "*Get out of my face.*"

Suddenly, Paul was lost in thought again, playing over in his mind the events that lead up to Juan rescuing him.

Earlier, another girl had shocked the class with her bold statement. The strange thing about it was that throughout the semester, this girl had gone virtually unnoticed. When Paul did look in her direction, she always seemed troubled, agitated, as if she was going through some crisis in life. And, oh yes, she was always writing something on her desk. And now, today, after three months of despondency, she dropped a bombshell. She raised her hand in what seemed like a desperate attempt to be heard, because she didn't even wait for the professor to acknowledge her, but defiantly proclaimed, "All my life my parents raised me to be a Christian. But after taking your class, professor, I no longer believe in Jesus or the Bible!"

What kind of sick, negative confession is that? Paul had thought. But before he could respond, it got worse.

"And now I argue with my mother and father day and night, to the point where we yell and scream at each other. Professor, won't you please come home with me and convince my parents that Christianity is a lie!?"

And then came the professor's response, the phrase that would haunt Paul and be his obsession for years to come. The words that came from the professor's lips should never be grouped together and spoken to a student in reference to their parents. What he said could be summed up in one ugly word. Violation!

How could he have said that? Does he not see what he's doing? Paul thought. *Surely no one could be that unprofessional. I have to speak to him.*

After class Paul made a beeline for the professor, past the strange girl still scribbling on her desk, past the students waiting to speak to their instructor, and lastly, past the beautiful girl.

"Professor, I need to talk to you about what you said today in class. I think you may have—"

Those were the last words Paul remembered speaking. The next thing he was aware of was a beautiful girl's perfume and her heated anger toward him.

As the events played in his mind, Paul stood frozen in thought. Again Juan snapped him back to reality, as if he were pressing ctrl+alt+del on a computer screen.

"Paul! You okay, amigo?"

"I feel so stupid," Paul exclaimed, his head still hung low. "I should have said something."

Juan quickly interjected. "Don't worry, man. Sometimes doing nothing *is* the right thing. Besides, if you had gotten into a yelling match with her, you would have destroyed your testimony before the class."

"Yeah, you're right," sighed Paul. But he could tell Juan was not satisfied with the response he gave him.

"So what now?" Juan asked.

Paul raised his head and answered. "I'll go home and plot the comeback." Juan smiled as Paul continued. "Ask God what should I do, and if I go forth, will I win the battle?"

Now Juan laughed. "Don't take this the wrong way, amigo. You *are* a fanatic. But I for one am glad you are." The two men embraced and said their goodbyes.

Paul sat in his room alone. He could hear the footsteps and voices in the hallway on the other side of the door, but he was lost in prayer and meditating on the day's events.

"He's an atheist," Paul said to himself while looking at the blank computer screen on his desk. "And he carelessly communicated his contempt for religion in a college class. Wow! That sounds good. Why couldn't I have said that today in class?"

The footsteps outside the door grew louder.

"He violated her!" Paul continued.

The voices outside grew louder too, but it did not distract Paul in the least.

"He violated her relationship with her family, with her God, and he violated her right to believe. The sad thing is, he doesn't even realize it. There has to be a way to show him what he's done, to let him know what he has taken from her. But how can I? They all think I'm some kind of religious monster."

Suddenly the door burst open.

BLAM!

For the third time today Paul was snapped back to reality.

"Daddy! Daddy!"

Paul's two children jumped up on his lap and greeted him with hugs and kisses. His daughter's name was Krysten, *Krysten Hope*. She was twelve and thought the world of her Father. Because she was a girl, her name, was a play on words. The *Christian's Hope* is Jesus. Every time he looked at his daughter's face, Paul would remember that and be encouraged. His son, PJ, was seven. His full name was Paul James. His parents had named him after Paul and James in the Bible. Also, he was named after his father and his uncle James who had passed away. These were good names, Christian names that communicated the loving bond they shared as a family; a bond that should never be broken.

"I want to tell him!" PJ yelled.

"No, I want to tell him," answered Krysten.

Paul stepped in to settle the great dispute.

"All right, what's so important that you both want to tell me?"

Krysten answered. "Mommy said dinner is ready!"

"And you have to come downstairs so we can pray!" added PJ.

Paul stared into his children's eyes as if a light just went on in his head. His heart would break if he could no longer enjoy something as simple as saying grace with his children.

That's it, He broke her sacred bond. Paul thought. *By teaching her to have contempt for God and religion, the professor has broken that young girl's sacred bond with her family. Where once, she and her parents may have prayed together, now with the bond broken, there was only hurtful arguments.* Paul had received his answer from God and knew now what he had to do. Don't *tell* the professor that he has violated that student; *show* the professor *how* he has violated her. Paul hugged and kissed his kids.

"Tell mommy I'll be down in a minute."

His children raced each other out the room and Paul turned to his computer and clicked on the green "F" icon on his desktop. Two weeks earlier his friend Taryn Atkins, an aspiring playwright, had offered him the script-writing program she had just purchased, *Final Draft*, for free. He now remembered her words when he told her he was not a writer.

"You never know if you'll need it." She had said.

"Yes," Paul said to himself. "This is bigger than me or the professor. If I make a film about this story, I can show the world how our religious freedom is being violated. It would benefit students, teachers, and parents. But what secular movie theatre would show—"

Paul stopped in mid sentence.

"No, not *theatres*, but *Churches*. Anyone holding the position that a student's belief system should be respected, could donate their talents and services toward making this film and it could be shown in *churches* across America. If done right, this could be the next great revival in the Christian world." Paul felt as if he were caught up in some greater divine plan. The revelation began to come fast and heavy like a large file being downloaded into Paul's mind by the fastest high-speed connection.

> *"The professor is only aware of his agenda, which is to communicate his hurt and anger toward God; but he is not aware of the hurt he is causing in return. The young girl who raised her hand earlier in class, the one who no longer believes, she is the focal point. Show him her life before she entered his class. Show him the treasured memories of a parent and child, the joy the family shared before he entered her life. Then show him that joy destroyed. There are many victims like her out there, children who have their faith stripped from them. Their stories go unnoticed. But I hear from heaven. Give her a name. Tell her story. This way you will help both student and teacher. All my children have a right to learn, but they also have a right to believe."*

Paul turned to his computer and began to type—

"T-H-E- M-I-S-E-D-U-C-A-T-I-O-N- O-F –J-O-Y."

Act I

Reflections of Joy

OPENING SCENE:

(On a black screen, a series of words begin to appear.)

The three most influential men that exist are:
The world leader, The religious leader, and...
The educator.
–Author unknown.

FADE TO BLACK

INT. CLASS ROOM: - MORNING

(Jim Byrnes, a college professor, sits alone in a classroom contemplating the recent events that have led him to reevaluate his teaching approach with his students. In one hand he holds an object unseen to the camera while flipping through the pages of a photo album.)

PROFESSOR BYRNES (NARRATOR)
I've been forced to ask myself a question recently, one that most educators so recklessly abandon, but should know the answer to before entering that classroom. *"What is the relationship between a teacher and his student?"* This is a question that is so often asked after something tragic happens. But by then it's usually too late.

(Professor Byrnes slowly runs his hand across the photographs in the album. His fingers stop at a little girl in a uniform, standing on the school steps, waving goodbye. The caption reads: "Joy's first day at school.")

PROFESSOR BYRNRES (NARRATOR) (Cont'd)
A student is defined as a learner who is enrolled in an educational institution. It is derived from the Latin word, "studere," which means to study. So, for all intents and purposes, a student is one who studies. The implication is that this person or *student* is moving on a path of education as he or she makes their way toward some future goal.

(Professor Byrnes lifts his head and looks at the empty seats around him.)

PROFESSOR BYRNES (NARRATOR) (CONT'D)
The chair. On the first day of school, the students come into class and sit in these chairs like incomplete products coming into my station on an assembly line. And we teachers are to fit them with the necessary piece they are missing that will prepare them for our secular world.

SHOT:(The camera moves down the row of chairs and stops at one student's desk in the back.)

PROFESSOR BYRNES (NARRATOR) (CONT'D)
That chair. As these incomplete products came and sat in these chairs, I would always ask them two questions. "What is your name," and "why are you here?" I would define these little incomplete products with a name. Let no one tell you differently, we teachers see students as little incomplete products defined by a name. But that is not what they are. If it were possible to see their lives before they entered your class, would it change the way you teach them? My God...*that chair.*

(Repeatedly carved into one of the desks attached to the chair are the words, "God please. Help my unbelief.")

PROFESSOR BYRNES (NARRATOR) (CONT'D)
Sitting in that chair was seventeen years of family values, memories, and beliefs.

(The professor turns his attention back toward the photo album. The picture on the opposite page is that of the little girl sitting upright in a hospital bed and smiling, surrounded by flowers and balloons that say "Get well soon." Beneath the picture are the words "Seven years of life." The professor runs his hands across the picture and then turns the page.)

PROFESSOR BYRNES (NARRATOR) (CONT'D)
You see, it's easy to do my job if I look at that chair as an assembly line; because then she was nothing more than an incomplete product, and my job was to help make her complete.

(The professor now looks at the last photo entry in the album. It is a picture of a young girl in a cap and gown hugging her parents. The caption reads "Joy's Highs School graduation.")

PROFESSOR BYRNES (NARRATOR) (CONT'D)
But if I see sitting in that chair *seventeen years*, then, my God, she is a person, not a product; who had been entrusted to my care, for me to help her in a specific area of education. And I could never make any of them complete. That was done a long time ago, by whoever created them.

FADE TO BLACK.

INT. HIGH SCHOOL AUDITORIUM - SIX MONTHS EARLIER
(Joy's high school graduation concludes with the graduates throwing their caps into the air. Afterwards, Joy runs over to her parents.)

JOY
Mom, Dad, I did it! I did it!

MRS. HUNTER (JOY'S MOTHER)
Yes baby, you did it. And your father and I are so proud of you.

MR. HUNTER (JOY'S FATHER)
Yeah, little girl, but you have someone else that's proud of you and has been with you all the way. God even helped you graduate early.

JOY
(smiling)
I know, Dad.

(Joy's teacher, Mr. Cramer, comes over to join them.)

MR. CRAMER
Are you Joy's parents?

PARENTS
(Speaking together)
Yes, we are.

MR. CRAMER
I am Mr. Cramer, one of the new English teachers here at the school. I just wanted to congratulate you and meet the parents who have raised such a wonderful girl.

JOY
(Hugging Mr. Cramer)
Thank you, Mr. Cramer.

(Joy's friends Holly and Samantha pull her away to take pictures.)

HOLLY AND SAMANTHA
Hi Mr. and Mrs. Hunter, hi Mr. Cramer.

HOLLY
Come on, Joy, let's go.

JOY
Bye, Mom, bye, Mr. Cramer.

(Joy runs off with her friends.)

MR. CRAMER
If we had more students like Joy in school, we instructors would teach for free. She is simply delightful. Mr. and Mrs. Hunter, You must tell me, what is your secret? How did you raise a girl with such a beautiful spirit?

MRS. HUNTER (JOY'S MOTHER)
Mr. Cramer, you're too kind. But truthfully, we really can't take much credit for Joy. We're just as amazed with her as you.

(Mr. Hunter puts his arm around his wife as she looks over at Joy talking with her friends.)

MRS. HUNTER JOY'S MOTHER (CONT'D)
Ever since she was a child, she was forced to see the harshness of this world.

MR. CRAMER
How so?

MRS. HUNTER (JOY'S MOTHER)
She was born very ill; but one day something beautiful happened that allowed her to see the same harsh world, but now, through hopeful eyes. It was as if she cared more about the condition of others than she did her own self. I don't mean to sound so somber, but the doctors told us she wouldn't live past her fifteenth birthday. We're just so grateful to God that she made it this far in life.

MR. CRAMER
So you can take credit, Mrs. Hunter, for showing her the beauty of life.

MR. HUNTER (JOY'S FATHER)
That's just it Mr. Cramer, it wasn't us. It was *God*. Her relationship with God governs her every move.

MR. CRAMER
Now I understand and your daughter has been a delight to have in my class. At the beginning of the school year, my wife was diagnosed with cancer, and one day I came to class late from the synagogue—

MRS. HUNTER
Oh, I did not know you were Jewish.

MR. CRAMER
Yes, the name often fools people, but anyway, your daughter saw I was depressed and came to me after class and I will never forget

what she said. She looked me square in the eyes and said "Mr. Cramer, there is no illness greater than Christ's love for your wife."

(Joy's mother is shocked.)

MRS. HUNTER
Oh! I hope you weren't offended.

MR. CRAMER
Pardon the expression, heavens no. I had been crying out to my God all morning in the synagogue. That's why I was late. And when she spoke, her words arrested me from my depression, and I remembered the prophet Isaiah. Chapters 61 and verse 3. "The spirit of the Lord is upon me to give them beauty for their ashes and the oil of joy for their mourning." This might sound crazy, but it was as if God was using your daughter to literally restore my joy. All I know is that she believed every word that she was saying to me and somehow I was no longer afraid.

MRS. HUNTER
You want to hear something just as crazy? We named her *Joy* after that very same scripture in your Bible. Isaiah 61.

(Mr. Cramer laughs.)

MR. CRAMER
Ha, ha, ha, "the oil of Joy." Of course. It all makes sense.

MRS. HUNTER
How's your wife?

MR. CRAMER
Oh, she's fine. She had a few treatments and the doctors said she is in remission. She's not out the woods yet, but she's doing just fine.

MRS. HUNTER
You are a wonderful teacher, Mr. Cramer, and I am glad my daughter knew you.

MR. CRAMER
You have a wonderful daughter and she will be a blessing to any instructor that has the pleasure of mentoring her.

MR. AND MRS. HUNTER
Thank you.

MR. CRAMER
Well, I have to go now; enjoy the rest of the day.

MR. AND MRS. HUNTER
You too, Mr. Cramer.

(Mr. Cramer walks off, laughing to himself.)

MR. CRAMER
Ha, ha, ha, "The oil of Joy."

CUT TO:
JOY AND HER FRIENDS

SAMANTHA
Joy did you hear anything yet?

(Joy pulls a letter from beneath her robe.)

HOLLY
Did you open it?

JOY
No. It came yesterday in the mail and I was too scared. I haven't even told my parents.

SAMANTHA
What!

JOY
What if I didn't make it in? All the other colleges I applied for turned me down.

HOLLY
That's because you weren't destined to go to those colleges, you were destined to go to *this one*, with us.

JOY
Yes, but I applied so late.

SAMANTHA
Are you going to open that letter or not?

JOY
You open it for me Sam.

(Samantha takes the envelope from Joy and opens it. After looking at the letter, she frowns.)

HOLLY
C'mon Samantha, what is it?

SAMANTHA
Dear Miss Hunter, after a careful review of your application to attend our prestigious college, we regret to inform you—

(Joy drops her head.)

SAMANTHA
That you will be spending the next four years with your two crazy friends at our college?

JOY
(Lifting her head)
What?

SAMANTHA
You've been accepted!

(The three friends scream)

HOLLY
The three of us together in college, this is going to be a blast. I can't wait.

JOY
Me either. I *sooo* want to be a Christian counselor. That way I can use Jesus to help as many people as I can.

SAMANTHA
Joy, you sound *sooo* corny. Just a minute ago, you didn't even think you were getting in.

JOY
(Hands in the air and spinning around)
I know. But I can't help it. God has been so good to me and I just want everyone to know it.

HOLLY
Calm down, girl. Save some of that for Sunday.

(Joy and Samantha laugh.)

JOY
Wow! College, this is going to be a new experience for me, for all of us.

SAMANTHA
That's right, girls. Next semester it's on.

JOY
(Looking at the acceptance letter)
I sure have a testimony for prayer service tonight. The doctors said I wasn't going to make it. But I'm still here!

(The three girls hug as another schoolmate passes by.)

SAMANTHA
Ooo, Tenisha. Take a picture of us.

(Holly hands Tenisha her camera and the three friends pose for the picture.)

-Click!-

JOY
Thanks, Tenisha.

(Tenisha walks off and the girls look at the picture in the camera.)

HOLLY
Now, that's what's up.

JOY
Yeah.

SAMANTHA
Wait. And whatever happens, you know we'll always be there for each other, right? Am I my sister's keeper?

SAMANTHA, JOY, HOLLY
Yes, I am!!!

HOLLY
We're going to college!

(The girls look at each other and scream.)

SAMANTHA, JOY, HOLLY
AAAHHH!

INT- DOCTOR'S OFFICE – AFTERNOON
(Joy and her mother are in the Dr. Foster's office waiting for him to return with the results of Joy's blood work and test results. Joy is behind the Dr.'s desk fidgeting with the draws.)

MRS. HUNTER
Get from behind that desk Joy. The Dr. is coming.

(Joy closes the draw, hurries back around the doctor's desk, and takes the seat next to her mother.)

DR. FOSTER
Good afternoon ladies. How are we feeling?

JOY
Blessed.

DR. FOSTER
I have your results here Joy.

(The Dr. sits down. As he places Joy's file on his desk, he notices a tract sticking out one of his medical books that says "Jesus Saves.")

JOY
So, are you going to come to church with me this Sunday Dr. Foster?

DR. FOSTER
Don't you want to hear the results of the test?

JOY
You're avoiding my question. Pleeeeze, come on Sunday.

MRS. HUNTER
I want to hear the results.

DR. FOSTER
All levels and tests are fine.

(Joy's mother sighs in relief.)

JOY
Two additional years of life and counting, Dr. Foster. Thanks to God.

DR. FOSTER
Yes, thank God. In fact, you're doing so well that I'm thinking about—

JOY
Getting rid of my medication?

DR. FOSTER
No, not yet. But we will reduce it.

(Dr. Foster opens his draw and reaches for his prescription pad. Inside, he sees another tract that reads "Jesus the Good Physician.")

DR. FOSTER
(Writing prescription)
You are persistent. I'll tell you what. You keep doing whatever it is you are doing to stay healthy and at your next check up in a few months; I'll come to church with you.

JOY
Deal.

INT. CHURCH - MORNING

(The Hunter family takes their seat in church. Joy retrieves her personalized Bible and sets it on her lap. Mrs. Hunter reaches into her purse and pulls out a small bag and gives the contents to Joy.)

MRS. HUNTER
Here baby, I picked up your new prescription from the pharmacy.

JOY
Thanks mom.

(Joy stares at the prescription bottle and her Bible.)

MRS. HUNTER
(Putting her arm around Joy)
Prayfully, one day you won't even need it.

PASTOR ROGERS
Before I attempt to encourage you with the word, is it all right if I
have a young lady come and encourage *me* with a song?

CONGREGATION
It's all right. Go ahead, Pastor.

PASTOR ROGERS
Come on up, Sister Joy, and bless us with a song.

(Joy places her Bible and medication on the pew between her parents and leads the choir in a song in which she thanks God for sustaining her. The congregation stands and cheers. As the song ends, Joy runs and embraces her parents and buries herself in their arms. On the pew, she notices her medication resting on top of her Bible. After staring at the two for a moment, Joy looks up toward heaven and smiles. Pastor Rogers begins to speak.)

PASTOR ROGERS (CONT'D)
My God. She couldn't even finish the song. Let's receive our
Bibles. The text for today is John 3:3. "And Jesus answered and
said unto him, Verily, verily, I say unto thee, except a man be born
again, he cannot see the kingdom of God." I have had many people
say to me, "Pastor, I am a good man. I don't lie, I don't drink, and
I don't steal. And as far back as I can remember, even from my
youth, I have always been a law-abiding citizen. Surely there is a
place in heaven for me?" And my reply has always been the same.
"Son, heaven is not a place like Bush Gardens. You just can't walk
up in there any time you like. Heaven is not a civic center or a park
open to the public. You can't wake up one morning and say honey,
pack up the kids, I feel like going to heaven. Heaven is somebody's
home. Lord have mercy. It is the self-designed domicile of God the
father and His Son Jesus Christ. And you can't get into someone's

house unless you know the owner. So, you may not be guilty of lying, cheating, or stealing, but if you walk into heaven without an invite from Jesus the Christ, you are guilty of trespassing.

(The elders stand to support the pastor as he preaches.)

PASTOR ROGERS (CONT'D)
If you try to sneak into heaven through the back door, by your good works, or through the side door, by your intellect, and not through the front door because you gave your heart to Jesus, then I don't care who you are, you're guilty of breaking and entering.

CONGREGATION
Amen! Amen!

PASTOR ROGERS (CONT'D)
Another woman said to me, "Pastor, I read the Bible, and I know every story in it. And I *think* I might be saved." My reply to her was "Daughter, being saved is like being pregnant. Either you are or you aren't. And just like you can't be a little pregnant, you can't be a little saved." We don't preach salvation through knowledge. We don't preach salvation through religion. We preach salvation through Jesus Christ. If you're down and depressed, he can lift you up. If you're sick in your body, he can heal you. If you're suffering... My God, if you're suffering? He can give you peace. Jesus is the way, the truth, and the life. And if you give your heart to him today, he'll set you free.

(The pastor finishes his sermon. Joy runs her finger across the inscription on her personalized Bible and then runs her finger across the label on her medication bottle. Both are engraved with her name.)

JOY
Mom did you hear what the Pastor said about suffering?

MRS. HUNTER
(Answering reluctantly)
Yes, dear.

JOY
Mom, I know God can heal you; but why do we suffer?

MRS. HUNTER
I don't know, Joy. Maybe God has some reason for it that we don't know about. You always ask that *same* question. Now, shh.

JOY
Dad.

MR. HUNTER
Yes Joy?

JOY
Why do people suffer?

MR. HUNTER
You with that again, girl? You heard your mother. Shh.

(Frustrated, Joy drops her head and stares at the two objects in her hand. Mrs. Hunter notices that Joy is upset.)

MRS. HUNTER
You okay?

JOY
It's just that I've been thinking about it a lot lately.

MRS. HUNTER
Yes, ever since your fifteenth birthday.

JOY
No, Mom. I mean even more. And I don't know why.

MRS. HUNTER
We'll ask the Pastor after service.

(Service ends and Joy and her parents walk over to meet with Pastor Rogers.)

PASTOR ROGERS
Melody, Dwayne. How are you doing?

JOY'S PARENTS
Fine, Pastor. God bless you.

MR. HUNTER
That was some sermon you preached today.

PASTOR ROGERS
Thank you for the compliment. I am glad you enjoyed it. And thank *you* Joy for the inspiration.

(Joy nudges her mother)

JOY
Ask him. Ask him.

(Mrs. Hunter taps Joy's hand away.)

PASTOR ROGERS
Joy, I want to congratulate you on graduating high school. I know you've had to overcome a number of setbacks in your life, so this is no small task. The church is very proud of you.

JOY
Thank you, Pastor Rogers.

MRS. HUNTER
Yes, Pastor. You have always been there for us and Joy, every time we needed you for prayer.

(Joy nudges her mother again. This time the Pastor notices it.)

PASTOR ROGERS
What is it, Melody?

MRS. HUNTER
Well, Pastor, Joy has a question.

PASTOR ROGERS
By all means, Mel, go ahead.

MRS. HUNTER
Well, Pastor, uhh…

PASTOR
The Bible teaches us ask and it—

JOY
I know God is good and everything, and can heal, but Pastor, why
do people have to suffer?

(The question catches Pastor Rogers off guard.)

PASTOR ROGERS
Huh, Well. Joy. There are some things we just should not ask about.

JOY
Why, Pastor?

MR. HUNTER
Because; if God wanted us to know, he would have told us. Right,
Pastor?

PASTOR ROGERS
Good point, Dwayne, but—

(Joy interrupts.)

JOY
It's all right if you don't know, Pastor.

MRS. HUNTER
(shocked)
Joy!

JOY
I have asked many people, but they weren't able to give me an answer. It's just something I've always wondered. That's all.

MR. HUNTER
All right now, Joy. Watch yourself. Proverbs 13:24.

PASTOR
It's okay, Dwayne. Joy, I have often wondered that myself. But that's not why I said you shouldn't ask the question. It is because, at this time, you may not be ready to understand the answer.

JOY
I'm not trying to be rude, Pastor, but that sounds a bit evasive.

MR. HUNTER
Proverbs 13:24, girl, Proverbs 13:24.

PASTOR ROGERS
(Chuckles)
Well, Joy, to be truthful with you, there is much about God and this world that I do not know. But in the many years that I have been a pastor, I have learned at least one thing when it comes to the subject of religion and God, and that is, there is the answer to the question that you have asked, and then there's the answer that you're truly looking for.

JOY
But isn't that the same thing?

PASTOR ROGERS
Ah, not always, Joy. It depends on what you're really asking. Why do people have to suffer? Or, why is it that *you* have to suffer?

(Joy drops her head and looks away.)

PASTOR ROGERS (CONT'D)
But enough of that. Like I said before, congratulations are in order. You graduated high school and now you are off to college. I'm very proud of you, Joy. You've always been an inspiration to me.

(Joy lifts her head.)

JOY
Me, Pastor? An inspiration to you? You always had to pray for me when I was sick.

PASTOR ROGERS
Joy, my praying for you was a formality. You've always had someone greater than me interceding for you. And one day you are going to learn what everyone whose life you've touched already knows.

JOY
What's that?

PASTOR ROGERS
That you are a gift from God, sent to help people who are struggling with their faith.

(Joy hugs Pastor Rogers.)

JOY
Ahhh. Thank you, Pastor.

PASTOR ROGERS
Throughout your life, you've fought and persevered, and despite your condition, you've never once doubted God.

(Joy's eyes well up with tears.)

PASTOR ROGERS (CONT'D)
In fact, I would like you to accompany me tomorrow, Joy.

JOY
Where, Pastor?

PASTOR ROGERS
To the, *Hands of Hope Foster Care Center*. God has arranged for us to help out as volunteers. They have children there who have also seen a lot of pain. Many of whom have been abandoned and I think your presence there would be a welcomed blessing.

JOY
Aw, Pastor, I'd love to but I have classes on Mondays.

PASTOR ROGERS
That's okay, Joy. Everything according to God's plan. If he wants you there, he'll make a way for you to be there.

MRS. HUNTER
Pastor, she does start school tomorrow. Would you mind praying for her?

PASTOR ROGERS
I would be honored. Everyone, everyone, stop for a moment wherever you are. Our sister Joy is going off to college, and we want to pray for her and all our graduates.

(The people stop moving as Pastor Rogers begins to pray for all the graduates but he cannot stop himself from praying particularly for Joy; the young girl who for some reason holds a special place in his heart.)

PASTOR ROGERS (CONT'D)
Father, in the name of your son, Jesus, You have placed a wonderful treasure in a little earthen vessel named Joy. And you've allowed her light to brighten our lives. Now, dear Father, as she and our other children go off to college, we pray that they will take with them all the virtues that we as parents have placed in their lives. We pray that wherever they choose to further their education, that they will both learn and be a light to all. May they do well in all that they endeavor to do. And, Father, stand with them in this the next stage of their life.

INTERIOR: THE HUNTER'S HOUSE - JOY'S ROOM. MORN-ING

(It is the first day of college classes. Joy is seated on the edge of her bed writing in her diary.)

—*I don't know how much time I have God; but from when I was little, I used to count every day I was alive. 6,287 days. That's 792 more than what the doctors gave me. But today is my first day of college. I think I will stop counting and just be thankful for the life you have given me.*— *Joy*

(Joy kneels at the foot of her bed and begins to pray. Her eyes are closed and hands tightly clasped. Her room is decorated with Bibles, family pictures, and other Christian items. A statuette of Jesus on the cross occupies her nightstand like a watchman. Hanging from the small statue is a gold cross edged in alabaster. As she prays, the narrator begins to speak.)

PROFESSOR BYRNES (NARRATOR)

What is the relationship of a professor and his student? Is it to restructure her mind as one would restructure a room? Like pictures on a wall, do we decide what ideas belong and what do not? Or maybe it is to re-create them in our own image, our own likeness, our own world view, or at least how we agree they should think. Come, get up off your knees little girl and sit in my chair, and I will tell you how you are to view the world.

(Joy gets up and takes the crucifix off the statuette. Its golden chain moves over her head and down her hair. The beautiful alabaster cross comes to rest softly on her chest above her heart. She then places her Bible securely in her book bag. The last item to be retrieved is her medication, which Joy reluctantly places in her bag. Before leaving, she closes out her computer. The screen saver changes between different Christian poems. The last one is Foot-prints in the Sand.)

INT. CLASSROOM IMEDIATELY FOLLOWING- DAY

(Students begin to pour into the classroom and fill in the empty chairs. Joy sits in one of the front seats, takes out her Bible, and places it on top of her history textbook. The professor writes his name on the blackboard, then turns to face the class.)

PROFESSOR BRYNES
Ladies and gentlemen, welcome to college. My name is Professor Byrnes and the class you are taking is, "History 110. Ancient Civilizations." We have a lot to cover and very little time to do so. But I must address a few things before we get started. The material we will be covering in this class is from prehistoric time to the beginning of the Roman Empire. And the terminology we will be using to date events in this class is B.C.E. and C.E. Does anyone know what these terms mean?

STUDENT 1
Before Common Era, and Common Era?

PROFESSOR BYRNES
Yes. Before Common Era and Common Era.

STUDENT 2 (FRANKIE)
What ever happened to BC and AD?

PROFESSOR BYRNES
I appall those terms. I find them grossly intolerant because they assume everyone is Christian. They disregard the possibility that one might adhere to a different belief system and they superimpose Christianity on us all. But I'm aware that a number of you have grown up with many of these religious words that have invaded our secular vernacular, and I will not hold you accountable if you use them.

(The professor takes out a book from his bag and strategically places it at the edge of his desk. The title reads, "The Illusion of God" A photo of a little girl sticks out from within the pages.)

PROFESSOR BYRNES (CONT'D)
In any case, in this history class, we will be discussing such topics as politics, racism, and, if you haven't already guessed, my favorite...religion. And because these are such controversial topics, I expect that some of you will be offended. We will be encountering a number of religions, some of which you may be familiar with. We will look at their origins, how they came to be, and we will be debunking many of the myths surrounding them. If you are overly sensitive and do not like to hear the truth, this class is not for you. For example, let's see who we can offend first. Did you know that the largest religion in the world today is based on an ancient Persian cult that dates back over three thousand years?

STUDENT 1
Professor, are you talking about Islam?

PROFESSOR BYRNES
No. Islam is the second largest religion in the world, with about one billion adherents.

STUDENT 1
So who's number one?

PROFESSOR BYRNES
Christianity is number one. In members that is. They have almost two billion professed members. And they are based on an ancient Persian cult called Zoroastrianism. Chapter six, in your textbooks.

(Joy places her Bible at the edge of the desk and stares at her text book.)

STUDENT 2 (FRANKIE)
So you are saying that Christianity is a cult? I thought it was supposed to be the only way to God.

(Joy opens her text book to chapter six and reads the heading. "Pagan influences on Christianity.")

PROFESSOR BYRNES
All religions claim to be *"the only way."* Christianity is just one of many. It's called exclusivity; and while Christians think they are following the practices of Jesus, they are really following the practices of a man named Zoroaster, who the religion is named after.

(Joy slams the textbook shut and accidentally knocks her bible off the table.)

Bam!

(The class stops to look at Joy and sees her Bible on the floor. Embarrassed, she picks it up and now places it under her textbook.)

PROFESSOR BYRNES (CONT'D)
Personally, I think it's quite arrogant for Christians to believe that they have a monopoly on the truth and exclusive rights to God. They believe they are right and everybody else is wrong. It is a bit more of a delusion than it is a revelation, and in this course, we will see that throughout history, people who follow religion, whether three thousand years ago or today, have always used their hearts to understand things, and not their heads.

(Joy retrieves her medication from her bag and squeezes the cross around her neck.)

(A student raises his hand.)

PROFESSOR BYRNES (CONT'D)
Yes?

STUDENT 3
Professor, that's not true.

PROFESSOR BYRNES
Are you offended?

STUDENT 3
No. But I do find you offensive.

(The class responds as if instigating a fight.)

CLASS
Oooo!

(Joy looks at the student and shakes her head in affirmation.)

PROFESSOR BYRNES
Well, the truth often is offensive.

STUDENT 3
Yes, professor, but so is a lie.

PROFESSOR BYRNES
What is your name?

(Joy looks at the student.)

STUDENT 3
Paul.

(The class begins to laugh. Frankie taps Joy, points at Paul, and laughs. Feeling pressured, Joy also smiles.)

PROFESSOR BYRNES
Ah, yes, the Apostle Paul. Are you a Christian, Paul?

STUDENT PAUL
(Looking around at the other students)
Yes, I am. And despite the sacrilegious laughter in this class, according to *your* figures on Christianity, I am not the only one.

(Joy looks at her cross.)

STUDENT 4
Chill out, man. It's just a course.

PAUL
You're wrong. It's not just a course. And we should have a degree of respect for God even when discussing Him in a history class.

(Joy raises her hand.)

PROFESSOR BYRNES
Yes?

JOY
Professor, I think Paul has a point. I took ancient history in high school and we never spoke about God like this.

PROFESSOR BYRNES
What is your name?

JOY
Joy.

PROFESSOR BYRNES
Well Joy, this is not high school and you're not in Kansas anymore.

(Joy looks around at the students as they laugh at her.)

PROFESSOR BYRNES (CONT'D)
Enough of this for now. We will have more time later to discuss the mysteries and the myths of Christianity. But I promise you I will do my best to be an equal opportunity offender.

STUDENT 1
What do you mean by that, Professor?

PROFESSOR BYRNES
I plan to offend all religions.

(The class laughs.)

PROFESSOR BYRNES (CONT'D)
In the time that is remaining, let us introduce ourselves to each other. When I point to you, I want you to tell me who you are and why you have taken this class.

(The professor points to Frankie in the front row.)

STUDENT FRANKIE
My name is Frankie Johnson and I really don't know what I want to do with my life. My mother told me to go to college or get a job. So, here I am. And to be honest, I took the course 'cause I need the credits. I thought it was going to be boring though, but today I have learned more about Christianity than I have in my entire life. I got to hand it to ya, Professor, you really know your stuff and you got me interested. I am really looking forward to seeing how all this religion stuff got started.

(Frankie looks over at Paul.)

STUDENT FRANKIE (CONT'D)
I always knew it was a bunch of junk. It just didn't make sense. How could a man come back from the dead?

PROFESSOR BYRNES
Like I said, we will cover Christianity later on in the course and when we do, you will see that there is little evidence that a man named Jesus ever existed.

STUDENT PAUL
Good Lord! Did I sign up for a history class or Atheism 101?

STUDENT 4
Calm down, man!

PROFESSOR BYRNES
Mr. Agard, the fact that I am sitting on this side of the desk and you are sitting on that side, proves that I know a little more about history than you.

STUDENT PAUL
Then, at what time in this course do you plan on teaching it?

PROFESSOR BYRNES
What's your major, Mr. Agard?

STUDENT PAUL
Education.

PROFESSOR BYRNES
And what do you plan to be?

STUDENT PAUL
A history teacher.

(Laughter again breaks out among the students)

PROFESSOR BYRNES
Well, you will make a lousy history teacher. You should think about changing you major.

STUDENT PAUL
Who are you to make that judgment call? History is a matter of knowing existing facts from the past, and there is more evidence for the existence of Jesus than there is for—

PROFESSOR BYRNES
I don't want to talk about it anymore. You have already used up enough of the class' time. Next.

(The professor points to Joy as Paul sits back in his chair, frustrated.)

JOY
My name is Joy Hunter and I would like to be a Chris—

(Not wanting to be mocked, Joy changes her words.)

JOY (CONT'D)
—uh, a counselor. And I am taking this course because I need the credits.

PROFESSOR BYRNES
Well, Joy, you have picked an honorable field. I am sure someone at home is proud of you.

(The professor moves on to the next student. Disappointed with herself, Joy again looks down at her cross and sighs. Class ends and the students exit the room, leaving only the empty chairs behind.)

EXT. SCHOOL BUS STOP: IMMEDIATELY AFTER

(Joy waits for her bus, still thinking about what happened in class. The narrator begins to speak)

PROFESSOR BYRNES (NARRATOR)
Two hours and forty-five minutes a week. That's all the time we have with your children. How can anyone expect us to teach them in two hours and forty-five minutes what it took historians ten thousand years to accumulate? That is an almost impossible task.

(Joy stares at the people across the street hurrying to their various destinations. Behind them is a gray-haired homeless man asking for something to eat; his outstretched hand captures her attention.)

PROFESSOR BYRNES (NARRATOR) (CONT'D)
What we *can* do in two hours and forty-five minutes is point them in what we believe to be the right direction. Introduce them to the secular world, and *influence* them. Yes, influence them.

(Joy walks over to the beggar and offers the hungry man some food. After sharing a lunch truck sandwich, Joy sits and reads to him from the Bible.)

PROFESSOR BYRNES (NARRATOR) (CONT'D)
Two hours and forty-five minutes may not be enough time to teach
them much, but it is more than enough time to influence your children.

*(Having fed the elderly man physically and spiritually, Joy boards
the bus for home. She looks out the window and smiles as her new
friend waves good-bye. After taking a seat on the bus, Joy looks at
the history book in her lap and a frown crosses her face.)*

E/I. JOY'S HOUSE. - EVENING.

*(Mrs. Hunter is in the kitchen preparing dinner as Joy enters the
house.)*

MRS. HUNTER
Joy!

JOY
Yes, Mom.

MRS. HUNTER
I'm in the kitchen, baby. Come on in.

JOY
Hey, Mom. What's for dinner?

MRS. HUNTER
Grilled salmon with those little red potatoes that you like. And for
desert, ice cream and cake. It's your first day at college, and I fig-
ured we'd celebrate.

JOY
Thanks, Mom, but I don't really feel like celebrating. In fact I don't
really feel like eating at all.

(Joy's father walks into the kitchen, clearly home from work.)

MR. HUNTER
Hey! How're my two favorite girls?

(Mr. Hunter lifts Joy up in a hug and spins her around.)

JOY
(smiling)
Daaad!

(Mr. Hunter puts Joy down and kisses his wife.)

MRS. HUNTER
Hey, babe.

MR. HUNTER
Mmm! Dinner smells good, baby. What is it?

MRS. HUNTER
Grilled salmon.

MR. HUNTER
Well, you know what the Bible says. He who findeth a wife . . .

MRS. HUNTER
Findeth a good thing?

MR. HUNTER
No. Findeth a good cook.

(Joy laughs and her mother hits her husband with a cooking spoon.)

MR. HUNTER (CONT'D)
Mmm. I see we have cake. What are we celebrating?

MRS. HUNTER
We *were* going to celebrate Joy's first day at college; but she was just telling me how she doesn't feel like celebrating, then you interrupted us with your corny jokes.

MR. HUNTER
What's wrong, baby girl? I thought you were looking forward to college.

JOY
Nothing, Dad. It's just that I wasn't prepared for what they talk about in these classes.

MR. HUNTER
Well, what do they talk about?

JOY
I guess it's not as much *what* they talk about as much as it is *how* they talk about it, you know what I mean?

MR. HUNTER AND MRS. HUNTER
No.

JOY
They talk about Jesus and how he may not have lived, how Christianity is a made-up religion and stuff like that.

MRS. HUNTER
What?

MR. HUNTER
Are all your classes like this?

JOY
No. Right now it's only this history course I signed up for.

MR. HUNTER
Well, tomorrow you can go down there and drop it. We're not paying a college thousands of *our* hard-earned dollars in tuition, to teach our children that God doesn't exist.

JOY
I just wish I could have been more prepared, more confident. I wanted to speak out but I didn't know what to say, the professor had an answer for everything. Or at least it seemed that way. I don't know, I kind of felt like I let Jesus down. Dad, you've been a Christian for a long time; what do I say when he tells me that Jesus did not exist?

MR. HUNTER
I don't know the answer to those kinds of questions, baby, but I do know what you can tell him. I am dropping your class!

JOY
No, Dad. I'm not a kid anymore. How am I ever going to learn to face challenges if I run from this one?

(Mrs. Hunter hugs Joy.)

MRS. HUNTER
I'm proud of you. I just wish we could be more of a help. The times seem to be changing so fast. Now everything is about what you can prove.

MR. HUNTER
Yeah. Just believe. That's the only thing that matters. All that other stuff is foolishness.

(Joy's mother taps her husband's chest lightly to calm him down.)

MRS. HUNTER
When your father and I were young, our world challenged us to be good Christians; but it seems like your world wants more. Your world wants you to give an answer.

MR. HUNTER
Well, I still think she should drop the class and forget about that nutty professor. It's a history class. If he wants to be an atheist, that's his business. She doesn't have to prove anything to him *or* change him. That's not her assignment. And if more of us Chris-

tians stood together on issues like this, these schools would think twice before pulling this kind of a stunt. You know what this is?

(Seeing that Mr. Hunter has taken the floor, the two women wait for the patriarch's answer.)

MR. HUNTER
It's . . . its secular peer pressure.

(The two women laugh.)

MR. HUNTER
What? What's so funny?

JOY
Don't worry, Dad. I won't even get involved in those stupid conversations. It's not even a part of my major. I'm just there to get the credits. Besides, I'm only there for two hours and forty-five minutes.

MRS. HUNTER
You're right. What's the worst that can happen? Feel like celebrating?

JOY
Yeah, Mom. You guys made me feel better.

(Still attempting to ease her father's mind.)

JOY (CONT'D)
Especially you, Daddy.

(Joy's father gives her a hug.)

MR. HUNTER
Always remember baby girl, it's God that controls your life, not some college professor. If the Lord wants to prove Himself to that man, then the *Lord* will choose His own vessel to do so.

CUT TO:
PROFFESOR. BYRNES' HOUSE

(Professor Byrnes comes home from work and enters his house. He turns on the light and hangs up his coat. His house is empty with only essential pieces of furniture filling the rooms. In the next room, a little girl's voice is heard calling out to her father. A dismal look crosses the professor's face. He ignores the voice, and moves on.)

CUT TO:
PROF. LIVING ROOM

(Professor Byrnes is seated in his living room. He retrieves his book from his briefcase and pulls a photograph from within its pages. He sits back and stares at the picture. The narrator begins to speak.)

PROFESSOR BYRNES (NARRATOR)
I went to an art show on campus once, and I fell in love with one of the paintings that was on display.

SHOT: *(THE CAMERA MOVES IN TO SHOW THE LITTLE GIRL'S FACE IN THE PHOTOGRAPH.)*

PROFESSOR BYRNES (NARRATOR) (CONT'D)
It so touched me that I stopped by every day after classes to see it. On the last day of the show I met the artist and asked him how long it took him to paint it. He said three months. For three months he would meet with his canvas. Once a week, and devote two hours and forty-five minutes to his masterpiece.

(The professor places the photograph back between the pages of the book and sets it on the coffee table.)

CUT TO:
JOY'S HOUSE

(The Hunters sits at the dinner table and Joy begins to pray.)

PROFESSOR (NARRATOR) (CONT'D)
Make no mistake about it. We as instructors see students as incomplete products, a canvas as it were, defined by a name. And each one of us, as teachers, is looking for that one student we can influence. That will be our masterpiece.

****

End of Act I

Chapter Two

Paul sat alone in the back of the lecture hall. From the top tier, he looked around at his classmates. His heart began to race. Five minutes ago, they had just finished the written part of their exam; now they each had to give an oral presentation.

"Mr. Agard, you're next," bellowed Ms. Lions from down in front of the hall.

Paul looked at the presentation papers in his lap. "Why did I take this class?" he whispered to himself. "Spielberg never went to film school; Tarantino never went to film school."

Paul could feel chunks of his presentation leaving his memory.

Yeah, but you're not Spielberg, he thought himself.

"Come now, Mr. Agard, Don't dillydally. Your classmates are waiting."

All eyes joined Ms. Lions' as she fixed her attention on Paul.

"You have five minutes to pitch your movie to us," she continued. "After which, we the producers will question you to see if your film is well thought-out. If it is, I will decide if you get the funding, or in this case, a passing grade."

Four tiers of seats separated Paul from the front of the class. As he passed each row, he could feel the stares of his colleagues, but there was no way of knowing their thoughts.

They're going to hate my presentation, Paul thought, as he passed the fourth tier. *How can I get them to understand?*

Tier three.

Turn your weakness into your strong point.

Tier two.

Open strong; don't be afraid of their faces.

Tier one.

Fix your face like flint.

Center stage.

"Good afternoon, ladies and gentlemen. My name is Paul Agard and the nature of my film today is pretty blunt, so my presentation will be also. The question before us is, "How do I get you, as investors, to reach into your pockets, and take out money to support my film?" Well, since we are being blunt, allow me to ask you a straight forward question. What if a professor ridiculed a student because she *did not* believe in God?

"Separation of church and state," Proclaimed a voice from the fourth tier. "She has the right to believe, or not!"

Paul now knew the thoughts behind their stares.

Ms. Lions snapped her fingers and motioned to the student in the fourth row to be silent.

"Thank you," Paul continued, now indicting Ms. Lions. "What if instructors like Ms. Lions, disrespected the young girl during class discussions, by not taking into account that what she was saying may be offensive to the student's secular beliefs?"

Chatter broke out in the lecture hall.

Third tier.

"In health class, we had to be respectful when speaking about sexual orientation in case there was someone in the class that had chosen an alternative lifestyle, the same should apply to a student's religious belief."

Second tier.

"Well since we're being blunt, I'll tell you right now, I would never support a film like that."

First tier

"Yeah, me either. It's too intolerant of other people's beliefs. In fact, I'd make a film the opposite of that."

Center stage.

"Students, he has five minutes for his presentation. Let him finish," Ms Lions demanded.

The students could feel the seriousness in the instructor's voice. Silence made its way up all five tiers till the murmuring stopped. Professor Lions now turned to Paul; there was no guesswork as to what she was thinking.

"By the way, neither I nor any other university professor would ever be so callous as to disrespect a student's sexual orientation or religious belief, and I must tell you Mr. Agard, you are hanging yourself with this strategy, both business-wise and academically."

Fix your face like flint, were the words that ran through Paul's mind one more time as he looked up at the student in the first tier.

"So you would not support a film like that?"

"No."

"And you, ladies and gentlemen, would give money to support a film that opposes religious intolerance in the educational system?"

The answer came from all four tiers and echoed off the walls in the lecture hall.

"Yes!"

"Well, let me tell you about *my* film…"

****

Act II

The Mis-Education of Joy

INT. CLASSROOM: - MORNING

(As class starts, Joy is one of the first students to enter the room. She walks past the first few rows of empty seats and finds a chair in the center of the class in full sight of the professor. The alabaster crucifix no longer adorns her neck and her Bible is no longer displayed on the desk. The other students enter the class, filling the seats around her, and Joy disappears from the professor's view.)

(Just as the Professor begins his lesson the door opens. Paul enters the class, notebook rolled up in his back pocket and a group of flyers in his hand. The heavy wooden door closes hard behind him.)

BLAM!

(The lecture stops. All attention is redirected to Paul who bares a massive red skull on the face of his black T-shirt. He stands at the front of the room long enough to find an open seat and to let the class get a good look at his shirt. As he makes his way toward the empty chair in the back, he places a flyer on the professor's desk. It is an invitation to a religious rights rally Paul is having on campus for the college's annual "Tolerance Day." Each student in Paul's path receives an invitation, after which they turn to look at him as he passes, including Joy. The final obstacle between Paul and his seat is Frankie, who has been waiting to ridicule him on his choice of shirts.)

FRANKIE
Red skull, huh? I collect comics too. It's the Punisher. A vengeful vigilante. Nice shirt, but not very Christian-like.

(A flyer lands on Frankie's desk and he also turns to look at Paul as he walks by. The back of his shirt reads, "I will punish sin—Isaiah 13:11" Frankie rolls up the flyer and discards it.)

PROFESSOR BYRNES
Mr. Agard. Kindly put away your Christian propaganda and take your seat.

(As the class gets underway, Paul and the professor get into a debate.)

PROFESSOR BYRNES (CONT'D)
Adam and Eve, the creation story, Noah's ark, are not real accounts. They are stories stolen from earlier Babylonian sources. And I am sorry, Mr. Agard, you may not want to hear this, but that which you call the *Word of God*, the Christian Bible, is nothing more than a bunch of myths, contradictions, and, in some cases, even lies.

(Joy places her hand on her chest and feels her heart racing inside her body. She reaches into her bag for her medication but instead grabs her cross and squeezes it tightly in her hand.)

PAUL
That's absurd! And quite frankly, Professor, I am surprised at your ignorance.

(The students react with shock.)

PAUL (CONT'D)
You stand up there and spit speculations as if they are truths. Even in a court of law you need at least two things for a conviction. One, hard or circumstantial evidence, and two, motive, and you, sir, have provided neither.

PROFESSOR BYRNES
You want motive? I'll give you motive.

(Joy covers her ears.)

PROFESSOR BYRNES (CONT'D)
After the death of their very human savior, the disciples did not want to look bad, so to give credence to their religion, they invented the resurrection story.

(Joy shuts out the argument until she only hears blurred sounds and not words. She reaches for her pen and begins to writing something on the desk.)

PAUL
And you have historical records that state this?

PROFESSOR BYRNES
No. You asked for motive.

PAUL
Are you a historian or the devil's advocate? I also asked for evidence, counselor.

PROFESSOR BYRNES
And you shall have it. There is not one contemporary document on Jesus in existence. The earliest extant copies we have were written long after his apparent life; three, four hundred years after his death.

PAUL
That's your evidence?

PROFESSOR BYRNES
It is.

PAUL
Then the devil has a poor lawyer. First of all, you are being purposely misleading, and taking advantage of the fact that my fellow students don't know anything about the subject. Second, some scholars have dated the New Testament writings as early as 45 A.D. and as far as the extant copies go, we have biblical copies such as p52 that date back to the middle of the second century. Some of these papyruses have been argued to be even older than that. Between 60 and 70 A.D—

PROFESSOR BYRNES
You're wrong! You're wrong!

JOY
(whispering to herself)
Why do you hate the Bible so?

PAUL
Okay. Let's say for argument's sake the extant copies date back to 300 A.D., like you said. These are still copies of copies that have been in circulation for some time. We have second century church fathers such as Polycarp quoting from New Testament books. This means the original writings—

PROFESSOR BYRNES
What's your point Mr. Agard? You are wasting our time.

PAUL
That's my point. You come across as this hard, callous man and you act as if God owes you something.

(The professor looks angrily at Paul.)

JOY
(Whispering to herself)
Yes, I've never met anyone so angry at God?

PAUL
In fact, since I've been in this class, I've never even seen you smile.

PROFESSOR BYRNES
Mr. Agard, I am surprised at you. At this point in the course, you should realize that the world is a very cruel place that does not leave you much to smile about. In fact, it has been my experience, that anything which makes you smile has a hold on you and therefore controls you.

PAUL
What?

PROFESSOR BYRNES
If you lose it, *that which makes you smile*, you lose a part of your self, and the resultant effect is pain, sorrow. So I try not to smile much.

(Joy unintentionally speaks out loud)

JOY
So you never smiled at a sunset, the color of a flower? Things that— Ah...

(She realizes her error too late.)

PROFESSOR BYRNES
Things that God has made, Ms. Hunter? Come now students, surely we can't be this naive. The world *has* no color, just existence. A rose does not know it is red and the euphoria that you experience upon looking at it exists only in your mind. But as I look into history and the world of men; the world which you claim *your* God has made, there are colors that I see, and am affected by. What is the color of war and of dying? What is the color of pain, sickness, and of human suffering?

(Joy stares at the medication in her bag and then at her desk which is covered with the words, "I believe—I believe")

PAUL
No God, no pain. Is that right Professor?

PROFESSOR BYRNES
Mr. Agard.

PAUL
Call me Paul.

PROFESSOR BYRNES
Paul. Spare me the psychoanalyzing. Since you do not want to adhere to history, I will use a more practical approach.

PAUL
And that is?

PROFESSOR BYRNES
Common sense. Does anyone in this room believe in the tooth fairy?

STUDENTS
No.

PROFESSOR BYRNES
Paul?

PAUL
No.

PROFESSOR BYRNES
Do any of you believe in the Easter bunny?

STUDENTS
No.

PROFESSOR BYRNES
Paul?

PAUL
No.

PROFESSOR BYRNES
Now, students, that I have Paul in line with the rest of the class, ask yourselves, why do you not believe in these things?

(Student 1 raises his hand.)

STUDENT 1
Ooo, I know; because they do not make sense. They are illogical.

FRANKIE
Just like the resurrection. Right, Professor?

(Joy looks at Frankie and then writes on her desk, "Help my unbe-lief.")

PROFESSOR BYRNES
There's a little more to it than that, but you are right; that is the basic idea.

PAUL
There's a lot more to it than that. The reason why you don't believe in those things has nothing to do with logic. It's because they were created to entertain and humor kids. They were never presented as truths. The stories in the Bible are put forth as historical accounts.

PROFESSOR BYRNES
So you don't believe in the tooth fairy?

PAUL
No.

PROFESSOR BYRNES
Why?

PAUL
Because it's a child's story.

PROFESSOR BYRNES
But you believe in Noah's ark?

PAUL
Yes.

PROFESSOR BYRNES
I rest my case.

(The student's laugh at Paul's response and Joy squeezes her cross tightly in her hand.)

PAUL
Well, allow me to cross-examine. Professor, do you believe that something can exist forever? That it can be eternal?

PROFESSOR BYRNES
What do you mean? Like the human soul?

PAUL
Whatever. Anything.

PROFESSOR BYRNES
I know where you're going with this, and the answer is no. Nothing can live forever, and the idea of your soul being eternal, a part of you living on after you physically die, is illogical. Just like the tooth fairy.

PAUL
So you don't believe?

PROFESSOR BYRNES
No. It's illogical.

PAUL
Do you believe in the law of conservation?

PROFESSOR BYRNES
Yes.

FRANKIE
The law of what?

PAUL
Go ahead, Professor, tell him what it is.

STUDENT 1
What is it, Professor?

PROFESSOR
(Clearing his throat.)
Ahmm. The law of conservation of energy. A law in physics that states neither matter nor energy can be created or destroyed. It is . . . eternal.

(Frankie looks angrily at Paul)

PAUL
Correct. Things are not eternal or true because man *understands* them to be so. Things are eternal or true because God has made them so. But your bias blinds you from seeing this. I'll ask you again. Do you believe that a thing can be eternal? Yes or no?

(The professor stares at Paul, but does not answer.)

PAUL (CONT'D)
You know what, Professor, don't even answer that question. I think we would all do better not to listen to you and read our Bibles instead. There! I rest *my* case.

PROFESSOR
Mr. Agard . . .

PAUL
Call me Paul.

PROFESSOR
No. I prefer to call you Mr. Agard. You are wasting a lot of our time with your Christian fanaticism and I have a class to teach, so we must move on.

(Joy looks over at Paul. She picks up his flyer and smiles.)

EXT-SCHOOL CAMPUS. - IMMEDIATELY AFTER

(Paul and a few of his friends are on the college lawn holding up signs and handing out flyers for their rally for Tolerance Day. They are joined by Joy, Samantha, and Holly.)

HOLLY
So, what are you doing?

PAUL
Protecting my First Amendment rights. These schools and colleges
get federal money yet some of them belittle religion and are insensitive to people's belief.

(Paul looks at Joy.)

PAUL (CONT'D)
You're in my history class, right?

JOY
Yes.

PAUL
Are you a person of faith?

JOY
Yes. I'm a Christian.

PAUL
How do you feel in Professor Byrnes class?

JOY
He's a very knowledgeable man.

PAUL
I didn't ask you that.

JOY
Uncomfortable… I feel uncomfortable.

(Paul looks at Holly.)

PAUL
I stand corrected. I'm protecting *our* First Amendment rights.

(Joy smiles and is given a sign that reads "I have the right to believe." As Paul continues to hand out the flyers, other students come over and question the group about their pamphlets and signs. Frankie is among the onlookers.)

STUDENT
(Opens a can of soda and takes a sip)
You got a right to believe what?

PETER – (STUDENT FROM PAUL'S GROUP)
What ever you want. As long as it's ethical and moral.

STUDENT
And who decides what's moral, *God*?

(A crowd starts to gather and Joy is noticeably nervous.)

STUDENT 2
Hey. Leave them alone. They're not bothering anyone.

STUDENT
Well they're bothering me. You Christians are all alike, going around judging people. What if I'm an atheist? Do I have the right not to believe?

PAUL
Yes, you do!

STUDENT 1
Well I think I'll exercise my right!

(The student throws his soda at Joy's sign and it spills on her too. Some of the other students laugh.)

FRANKIE
Where was your God? Why didn't he protect you from that?

INT. COLLEGE CAMPUS-GIRLS BATHROOM. - IMMEDI-ATELY AFTER

(Joy stands at the sink, cleaning the soda off her face and clothes. But as much as she scrubs, she still feels the sticky substance on her skin. Her heart races out of control as Frankie's words play over in her head.)

"Where was your God? Where was your God?"

JOY
Where are you Lord?

(Frankie's words are suddenly replaced by the voice of Joy's father as she remembers sitting on his lap as he tells her about the day she was born.)

JOY'S FIRST MEMORY FLASH BACK:

INT. HOSPITAL. - EVENING

(Mrs. Hunter is in the premature section of the hospital's nursery. She is standing behind the glass looking at the frail body of her new born. The child is underdeveloped and fighting for its life inside an incubator. A tall, broad-shouldered man approaches Mrs. Hunter and begins to encourage her.)

STRANGER
It must be hard for you.

MRS. HUNTER
It is.

STRANGER
Hi. My name is Gabriel.

MRS. HUNTER
Like the angel?

STRANGER
(Smiling)
Yes, like the angel. You must be a Christian.

MRS. HUNTER
Yes. How did you guess?

STRANGER
I've introduced myself to a number of people in this ward, but you're the only one that called me an angel.

MRS. HUNTER
Are you a doctor?

STRANGER
No, but I work for one.

MRS. HUNTER
So I guess you've seen a lot of suffering children?

STRANGER
Yes, but I've also seen a lot of miracles.

MRS. HUNTER
Are you a Christian?

STRANGER
(Smiling)
No. I am not a Christian.

MRS. HUNTER
It's still hard though, watching her suffer.

STRANGER
Can I give you a word of encouragement?

MRS. HUNTER
If you'd like.

STRANGER
She was born in sorrow, but maybe like your savior, she will bring the world joy.

(Mrs. Hunter turns to look at the man and then at her child. She then turns and walks back to her room where the doctors are speaking with her husband.)

DOCTOR
Your daughter is extremely sick, Mr. Hunter.

MR. HUNTER
Will she be all right doctor? Will she live?

DOCTOR
We are doing our very best, Mr. Hunter. I really mean that. But we may have to prepare for the worst. She's extremely underdeveloped. In fact it's a miracle she's even lived this long.

MR. HUNTER
Jesus . . .

NURSE
Mr. Hunter, she still doesn't have a name. Maybe if you chose a name for her, it would help take your mind off things.

MR. HUNTER
I don't even know if she's going to live. I wouldn't know what to call her.

(Mrs. Hunter walks in the room.)

MRS. HUNTER
Joy. Her name will be Joy.

(Back in the campus bathroom, Joy responds to the memory with a smile. She can feel her heart rate begin to slow down as she recalls yet another memory.)

JOY'S SECOND MEMORY FLASHBACK:

INT. THE HUNTER'S HOUSE -BEDROOM. - EVENING

(A three-year-old Joy is suffering with a high fever. Her parents fight to get it under control. They call Pastor Rogers over to pray for Joy, but he is also struggling with his own issue of doubt.)

MRS. HUNTER
Dwayne, she's burning up.

MR. HUNTER
What's her temperature?

MRS. HUNTER
104.

MR. HUNTER
She's been like this for three days now.

MRS. HUNTER
Yes. But it wasn't this high. Did you call the pastor?

MR. HUNTER
Yes. His wife said they'll be right over.

MRS. HUNTER
I don't know, Dwayne. She doesn't look good and she's not moving much.

MR. HUNTER
I'm getting my coat. We're taking her to the hospital.

(The doorbell rings. Mr. Hunter opens the door. Pastor Rogers and his wife have come to support the Hunters.)

MRS. ROGERS (PASTOR'S WIFE)
How is she?

MR. HUNTER
I'm taking her to the hospital, she doesn't look good.

(Joy's mother walks in to the room.)

MRS. HUNTER
No. Let Pastor pray for her first.

MR. HUNTER
Baby, we don't have time for that. She may be—

MRS. HUNTER
What! Dying? Let Pastor pray for her Dwayne. Please.

MR. HUNTER
Mel. Baby . . .

PASTOR ROGERS
Dwayne's right, Melody. She's had two surgeries in three years, the doctors said this could happen; and I don't know...I just don't know.

MRS. HUNTER
You don't know what? If God is strong enough?

(Pastor Rogers looks away; and his wife places her arm around his shoulder.)

MRS. ROGERS
He's been having some doubts lately, Melody. He was going to tell the church this Sunday, that he was stepping down from the ministry.

MRS. HUNTER
Pastor?

PASTOR ROGERS
I don't know if *my* faith is strong enough, Mel.

MRS. HUNTER
Well, mine is. Please Pastor. Pray for her. Pray for my Joy.

PASTOR ROGERS
(Whispering to his self)
God, my faith is weak. Please, give me a sign—

MRS. HUNTER
Pastor?

(Pastor Rogers gathers the others, closes his eyes and prays.)

PASTOR ROGERS
Father, we need your help tonight. There is a little girl who we all love, suffering in the next room. I don't have the power to heal her, and...my faith...

MRS. ROGERS
It's OK, Dear.

PASTOR ROGERS
If you heal this little girl tonight, I will never doubt you again.

(In her parents' bed, Joy is drawn to the voices in the next room.)

PASTOR ROGERS (CONT'D)
Please father, extend your healing hand tonight, in the name of Jesus...

(After praying for a few moments, Pastor Rogers no longer hears the response of the others. He opens his eyes to see why they are quiet and finds young Joy standing in the circle in front of him. He picks her up and holds her in his arms.)

PASTOR ROGERS
My God, she's soaking wet.

MRS. ROGERS
(Feeling Joy's head)
But her fever's gone.

(Pastor Rogers tries but cannot hold back the tears.)

PASTOR ROGERS
(Looking up to heaven)
I will never doubt you again.

CUT TO:
JOY BACK IN THE COLLEGE BATHROOM

(Joy smiles, as she touches her chest. Her heart beat has returned to normal. From out in the hallway, her two friends call to her.)

SAMANTHA
(Opening the bathroom door)
Joy! Joy!

HOLLY
Hey, girl, you *still* in here?

JOY
What's up?

SAMANTHA
We've been waiting outside for you for a minute. You sure you're all right?

JOY
Yeah, I'm okay.

(Seeing Joy's clothes wet and her sleeves rolled up, her friends try to make light of the soda incident.)

HOLLY
(Looking in the mirror)
You like my hair? I had to switch it up since I got soda in it too.

JOY
Holly, you know you always look good.

SAMANTHA
Don't lie to the girl, Joy. Anyway, I hope that guy didn't mess with your head.

JOY
I don't know. I can't even think straight right now. I got a lot on my mind.

HOLLY
Me too; I got a lot of studying to do. I have a test tomorrow, so let's get out of here. I don't think I'm going be able to make it to prayer group tonight.

SAMANTHA
Oh no you don't! If you have a test tomorrow, that's all the more reason you should come out for prayer. But, forget you. What's wrong, Joy? Is it about what happened today?

HOLLY
Yeah, Joy, what's up?

JOY
What happened today, this history class I'm taking. I don't think I am ready for this.

HOLLY
I know what you mean, sis. It's a lot of work. But weren't you the one that was looking forward to going to college?

JOY
(Smiling)
It's not the work, you guys. It's this history teacher and the stuff that he talks about in class. I'm telling you I am not ready for this.

HOLLY
Well, what does he talk about? History and the properties thereof?

JOY
I wish. He talks about did Jesus really live or was he a myth.

SAMANTHA
What?

HOLLY
In a history class?

JOY
Yeah. And he said some of the stories in the Bible are no truer than the tooth fairy and the Easter bunny.

HOLLY
He needs prayer.

SAMANTHA
No. He needs Jesus.

HOLLY
So what did you say when he said all that?

JOY
What could I say? I don't know the answers to that. Paul's in my class and he's always arguing with the professor, but everyone thinks he's a fanatic. And you saw what happened today. I don't want that happening to me again.

SAMANTHA
I know. We'll let the pastor meet him. He'll know what to say.

JOY
No! I asked Pastor a question about God, and he didn't even know the answer to that. This professor will eat him alive.

HOLLY
So what are you going to do?

JOY
I don't know. But the problem is not me in the class. It's the class in me. When I leave, I keep hearing the professor's words in my head. *"Is Jesus real?" "The Bible is a lie!"*

SAMANTHA
Forget the professor! Girl, you need prayer. We're going to hang out with you for the rest of the day. But first we have to stop by Hands of Hope.

HOLLY
The orphanage? That's not hanging out.

SAMANTHA
I know. I have to pick up something for the church. Then we can hang out and go to prayer meeting tonight.

HOLLY
Prayer meeting? I told you I have a lot of studying to do.

SAMANTHA
Yes, prayer meeting. You need prayer most of all. Walking out here with your hair looking like that. What's wrong with you? Besides am I my sister's keeper?

HOLLY
(looking at Joy)
Yes I am.

(Joy smiles)

INT. CHILD CENTER - IMMEDIATELY AFTER.

(Joy and her friends enter the child center and are greeted by the receptionist.)

RECEPTIONIST
Good afternoon, ladies, may I help you?

SAMANTHA
Yes. My name is Samantha and we are from Christ Temple, Pastor Rogers. And we are here to pick up the information package for the church.

RECEPTIONIST
Oh, yes. I'll go get Mrs. Washington. Please wait inside and make yourself comfortable. I'll be right back.

(The girls enter a large room where the children are stationed in front of rows of easels. The children chat playfully as they paint. On the other side of the room, Joy notices a little girl by herself staring out the window. Next to the girl is a table with toy dolls and flowers. Joy walks over and begins speaking to the little girl.)

JOY
Hey. What'cha doing?

LITTLE GIRL
(turns to answer Joy, then looks away again.)
Looking out the window.

JOY
What's out there?

LITTLE GIRL
I don't know. I only know what's in here.

(Back across the room Mrs. Washington walks over to meet Samantha and Holly.)

MRS. WASHINGTON
How are you doing? I'm Mrs. Washington. Here's the information Pastor Rogers wanted.

(Joy continues talking to the little girl.)

JOY
What's your name?

LITTLE GIRL
Ahdi.

JOY
Why aren't you with the other kids? Don't you like to paint?

AHDI
Yes I do. I used to paint a lot before I came here.

JOY
So why won't you play with the other kids, Ahdi?

AHDI
Because we won't be friends for very long.

JOY
Why not? Are they being mean?

AHDI
No, most of them leave.

JOY
That's even the more reason why you should be over there playing with them. You all might be leaving soon.

AHDI
(Turning toward Joy)
No, I said they leave. I always stay.

(Ahdi turns her head back and stares out the window.)

SAMANTHA
Thank you, Mrs. Washington.

MRS. WASHINGTON
You're welcome.

SAMANTHA
Holly. Where's Joy?

HOLLY
Over there, with that little girl.

MRS. WASHINGTON
Ah, I see your friend has met Ahdi.

HOLLY
I noticed her too when we walked in. Mrs. Washington, why is she over there by herself?

MRS. WASHINGTON
Ahdi has a special personality for a little girl.

HOLLY
Is she okay? Is she depressed?

MRS. WASHINGTON
No, nothing like that. She just had a few hopeful couples back out on her and now she's developed a hard shell. Rejection is especially hard for these children, and sometimes they develop coping mechanisms. But she is one of the brightest girls in the agency. And if you speak to her for more than five minutes, you would find that out.

SAMANTHA
Joy! Come on. Let's go.

(Joy turns to answer her friends and then continues speaking to the little girl.)

JOY
I'm coming; just give me a moment.
Well, Ahdi, I'm your friend.

AHDI
If you say so.

JOY
Can I tell you a story, Ahdi?

AHDI
Sure. And then you have to leave, right?

JOY
(Smiling)
Hmmpfh. Can I tell you a story?

AHDI
Yes. You can tell me a story.

JOY
Once there was a great king who cared for all his subjects. So he went into his royal garden and picked out the most beautiful flowers to give them. He then went into the houses of all the people in his kingdom that were sad, and gave them each a flower to place in their homes. And each time they saw the king's flower, no matter what situation they were in, they always knew everything would be all right. Do you know why?

AHDI
(Smiling)
Because the flower made their homes pretty?

JOY
That's right; and because the flowers reminded them that the king cared for them and this gave them hope. Do you know what the moral of the story is?

AHDI
What is it?

JOY
Well, in the story, God is the great King and the flowers are special people that he has sent into the world to encourage those who are sad. And the moral is, in life you can either be someone who is sad or you can be a flower.

(Joy pulls one of the toy flowers that was on the table from behind her back and give it to Ahdi.)

JOY (CONT'D)
Which one are you?

(Ahdi smiles and takes the flower.)

AHDI
I'm a flower.

(Joy hugs Ahdi.)

AHDI (CONT'D)
That was a good story. You made me feel better. What's your name?

JOY
Joy. My name is Joy.

AHDI
Joy, you're a flower too.

(Joy kisses Ahdi on the forehead.)

JOY
Takes one to know one. I gotta go. I'll see you soon.

INT. MALL - IMMEDIATELY AFTER

(Joy and her friends go to the mall. They shop, laugh, and avoid advances from boys. As they stop to eat, an elderly woman sitting alone drops her tray and the three girls eagerly rush over to help her. Afterward, Joy returns home and finds her parents have invited Pastor Rogers over to pray.)

JOY
Pastor!

PASTOR ROGERS
Your mother told me you were feeling bad about one of your classes, so I came right over.

JOY
I was, earlier; but not any more. Pastor, I have got to tell you about this marvelous day I had. I went to the mall with my friends. We ministered to this nice lady, and we went to prayer—

PASTOR ROGERS
(Laughing)
Joy, you really have a divine hand watching over you. This is yet another time I have come over to pray for you and found that the Lord has been here before me.

(Joy's hugs her pastor.)

PASTOR ROGERS
You've always made my job easy, but do you mind if I pray for you anyway?

JOY
No, Pastor.

(As the Pastor prays, the narrator speaks.)

PROFESSOR BYRNES (NARRATOR)
Beautiful moments in life cannot be destroyed. They have happened... they are forever. Anything from a laugh shared among friends to the relationship between a young girl and her spiritual leader. But what if you had the power to indirectly affect these moments? Hmm. Teachers. Every instructor teaches for a reason. Whether it's because they love their craft, or because life has left them no other alternative. But no matter the reason, every educator at one point in their career has said to themselves, *"Maybe I can make a difference by changing their lives."* But to what extent? How they act? What they think? How about what they believe? An

educator must be careful to change a child's life for the better, with out tarnishing the beauty in their past. Beautiful moments in life cannot be destroyed. They have happened…they are forever. But they can be tarnished.

****

~ End of first half ~

~Intermission ~

Chapter Three

Paul hurried up the stairs as fast as he could.

"Come on Juan. Hurry up," he called back to his friend.

"I'm moving as fast as I can, amigo," Juan shouted from behind him.

"C'mon, if I don't get this paper in today, Byrnes is gonna hang me." But Juan could not keep up, Paul was covering two, three steps at a time now.

"Go ahead, Pablo. I'll meet you…"

Paul never heard the rest of the sentence. Juan's voice faded as the distance between the two friends grew greater.

Blam!

Paul burst through the door of the fourth floor staircase in the Madison building on the college campus. His eyes searched the beautiful hallways decorated with archeological artifacts from around the world, proudly displayed behind glass cases. To his right there was a room with an open door and voices could be heard coming from inside. To his left was a set of offices behind a glass door with a large number above it.

"There," Paul said out loud. "Room 402. Ancient History Department."

Even from down the hall Paul could see that most of the offices were in darkness inside the history department, but there was still one light on and the main door was not shut.

"Yes," Paul said. "It's still open."

He hurried down the corridor, as he did; the archeological displays and their captions became much clearer.

"Australopithecus: Early Hominids Ancestors of Humans.

Afarensis :Lucy: Early Bipedal Ape.

Africanus:Taung Child: Intermediate Between Humans and Apes."

Beautiful reconstructions of what the fossils might have looked like challenged Paul from behind their glass cases. One display pictured how the creatures would have lived in their environment and showed two apes walking upright, side by side with the male's arm affectionately draped over the female's shoulder. Paul read every caption and stored them in his mind. This would be a fight for another day.

As Paul neared the office, the last light in the office went out and Professor Byrnes stepped out into the hallway, turning slightly to close the door.

"Professor Byrnes. I have my term paper," Paul said anxiously.

Professor Byrnes, unfazed, set his briefcase on the floor and searched for the keys to the department door.

"It's late. I said get it to me before the end of my office day, and as you can see, my office day has ended," Professor Byrnes said, smiling contently.

"Not technically, Professor," Paul quickly responded. "You may have turned out the light, but you have not shut the door. There's still hope for you—uh—for me yet. To turn in my paper, that is."

Professor Byrnes stared at Paul, his smile turned to a frown as he shut the office door and locked it sternly.

"Half a letter grade," he responded coldly as he took Paul's paper and turned to walk away. "And your paper better be good."

Paul followed his instructor down the hall, thanking him continually. As they neared the teachers' lounge, the voices from inside grew louder and the words became more distinct. The incensed Professor stopped in front of the open lounge door.

"Now, if you are finished, there might still be *hope for me* to eat lunch."

The Professor entered the room, opened the closet door in the lounge corridor, and hung up his coat, leaving Paul outside in the hallway to feel the coldness of his sarcasm. A smile returned to the professor's face as he looked back to see the proud student's head drop slowly. Paul stood in the doorway until Professor Byrnes disappeared into the inner room of the teacher's lounge.

"Yes! Check and mate," Paul said; elated with himself for just barely getting his paper in. Alone now, Paul could hear the discussion going on inside the room. He bent his head forward to hear the voices.

Blam!

Paul jumped. Down the corridor from out of the staircase sprang Juan; out of breath and buckled over.

"You owe me, amigo," Juan said as he made his way toward Paul.

"Man, where were you? I've been here for about five minutes."

"Mida! I was all the way... on the sixth floor.... You left me and I didn't know... where to go," Juan replied, between pants.

The two friends laughed and Juan grabbed his side from pain and humor.

"¡Ay, el dolor," Juan said between laughs and pants.

"Quiet, Juan, stop breathing so hard,"

"What are you doing?" Juan inquired as he straightened up. "Eavesdropping?"

"No. That would not be right."

"So what are you doing?"

"Reconnaissance."

The two friends bend their heads forward to hear the voices in the room.

"We need a new science curriculum in our schools and that's what I would petition this college to establish," said one of the voices in a confident tone, each word slow and pronounced.

"A new science curriculum!? a next voice objected sharply, which Paul and Juan quickly identified as Professor Byrnes.

"Hank, the age of Bible ethics and traditional Christian values is over," proclaimed a third voice, in a cold and sarcastic tone. "We are a secular nation, run by a liberal government; and conservative ideologies like yours are a thing of the past. Take a look at our new president."

"Well, that's where you're wrong. President Obama has promised to be a president for all of us and I am willing to give him the opportunity to do so," Hank replied, his words becoming even more pronounced.

Inside the room, Professor Byrnes pours three cups of coffee and places two of them on the table in front of his colleagues.

"Dean's right, said Professor Byrnes. "Biblical politics has slowed this nation down for too long. In any case, putting peoples hopes in religion and God only end in despair. We've had enough of conservatism. I like Obama's liberal approach. He's not afraid to open up stem cell research. If we had more presidents like that, maybe we could have helped..." Professor Byrnes pauses for a moment and stares at the cup cradled in his hands. "Well, we can do a lot of good *now*."

Dean stirs his coffee slowly and stares at his nemesis seated across from him.

"Tell me, Hank, and what exactly would you change? Would you do away with evolution and the empirical sciences and replace our textbooks with your Bibles?" Dean said mockingly.

"That's just my point. Parts of the evolutionary model are neither empirical nor good science," Hank quickly replied. "Evolution as it stands, describes genetic changes in an organism, from generation to generation. I have no problem with that. In fact, that type of evolution is verifiable."

"And?" Dean asked sarcastically.

"*And.* The mechanisms of these changes are said to be natural selection, genetic drift, and mutations—"

"So what's the problem?" Interjected Professor Byrnes.

"The *problem* is, *Macro* evolution. In our textbooks, we are told that whales evolved from some hyena-like mammal, birds from reptiles, and humans from apes. These conclusions are not based on *verifiable testing* but are speculations based on *inferred similarities* in the *fossils* of these creatures."

"Some of which we have displayed in the very hallways of this building. What's your point?" Professor Dean replied, now taking a sip of his coffee.

"For one, natural selection is not enough to prove *that type* of evolution has occurred. By definition, it is nature selecting *existing* organisms to survive; not nature *evolving* existing organism. Second, we have no DNA from these extinct species to compare with their evolutionary predecessors or progeny. All evolutionary relationships are established based on suggested similarities in their fossils; and where we do have DNA, we can only prove distinction, not transition. And finally, there is no scientific test that observes a series of mutations that leads to macroevolution. That part is all speculation and guess work. All methods of science are either silent on the subject of evolution or *scream* contradiction. You can't claim, Natural selection and mutation, is the testable mechanism for evolution" and then use, Paleontology, as your proof. In science your claim must be proved within your hypothesis. It's a sleight of hand that evolutionists pull. But Christianity has always been skeptical when it comes to evolution."

"And your proposed change, sir?" Professor Dean asked condescendingly.

"A curriculum based on observable and proven science. This is not the eighteen hundreds. Evolution is an outdated theory. We now know how living organisms are formed. *DNA*. Let's teach biology based on that. Before the 1950s, evolution was a study of existing or extinct organisms and we speculated as to how they were formed. With the discovery of DNA the guesswork is over. Genetic instructions on a nucleic level forming distinct living and functional creatures. It all but removes the question; *"Did one species evolve into another?"* Because each new generation is a copy of the first. That is the observable mechanism in DNA."

"And what should we call this new curriculum? Intelligent design?"

Professor Hank set his cup on the table and leans forward to answer.

"Every textbook on evolution describes DNA as instructions, information, blue prints, and codes. And if two sets of bones separated by millions of years can be used to conclude common ancestry, then instructions and information can be used to conclude intelligence."

"Yes!" Paul cried from outside in the hall.

The three professors stop and looked at each other. Professor Byrnes rushes to the door and peers into the hallway. After looking left and then right, he heads back to the inner room and closes the door.

"No one there," said Professor Byrnes, shrugging his shoulders.

"Must have come from down the hall," Hank said.

"It's been an interesting chat, gentlemen, I am curious as to how Obama or even the college would respond to such a suggestion," Professor Dean said as he placed his empty coffee cup on the table. "But as for you, Hank, I would love to have one of your biology students sit in my Philosophy of Religion class and spew that fundamentalist nonsense. I would, uh . . . dissect his argument and send him back to you. Excuse the pun."

In the lounge hallway, the closet door opens slightly and two figures step out and make their way quietly toward the staircase.

"Man, that was close," Paul said in relief.

"Yeah, next time you eavesdrop, you're on your own."

"Reconnaissance, Juan. Not eavesdropping, reconnaissance."

"So what do you think amigo?"

Paul looked at his friend and smiled.

"I think it's time to sign up for next semester. *Philosophy of Religion.* Hmm."

****

Act III

-The Loss of Joy-

EXT. SCHOOL CAMPUS: FOLLOWING WEEK

(Joy and her friends are walking on campus before their classes start.)

JOY
Today's different.

HOLLY
Yeah. It's Monday.

JOY
No silly, I mean me. I'm different. I've got to stand up for what I believe.

SAMANTHA
How so, Sister Soda?

(Holly giggles)

JOY
If I'm ashamed to speak up for Him before men, He'll be ashamed of me before God.

SAMANTHA
What does that mean?

HOLLY
It means next time someone throws a soda at her, she'll duck.

(Samantha and Holly laugh.)

(Joy notices Frankie in front of the student hall building where the different campus clubs meet.)

JOY
Follow me.

HOLLY
Over there? Joy, no! I was only kidding.

(Joy begins walking toward Frankie, who is talking with his friends as they enjoy a cigarette. Holly and Samantha hurry after Joy.)

SAMANTHA
Wait—

(As the girls get closer, Frankie and his friend's conversation become clearer and obscenities can be heard between breaths of cigarette smoke.)

JOY
Hello, Frankie.

FRANKIE
Hey, Joy. So nice of you to join us real people. You lost or something?

JOY
No. But you are.

FRANKIE
Well, it seems like Dorothy has found some nerve. Who're your two friends?

JOY
Scarecrow and Tin Man.

(Frankie's companions laugh.)

JOY
I want to talk to you about what happened last week. I have your answer.

(Frankie ignores Joy's address.)

FRANKIE
Let me introduce you to my friends. This is Richard. He's into Goth.

(Richard is a tall, menacing lad with pitch black hair, pale white skin, and clothed in dark apparel adorned with pins and buckles. A stainless steel pentagram hangs proudly from his neck. Joy notices the black polish on his nails as he raises his hand to his mouth and takes a deep drag of his cigarette. After extending his neck upward to expel the thick white smoke from his lungs, he speaks.)

RICHARD
Charmed.

FRANKIE
Next we have Kevin, but he likes to be called lace, for obvious reasons.

(Kevin is a strikingly handsome young man dressed in tight straight leg jean a rainbow colored belt, white T-shirt and sneakers. On his right hand he sports a black lace glove.)

KEVIN
(Extending his hand)
Pleased to meet you.

(Joy takes hold of Kevin's hand; but the three girls are drawn to his flawless make up and the thick black liner that perfectly outline his eyes.)

HOLLY
(Whispering to Joy)
His make up looks better than mine.

(Joy elbows Holly.)

JOY
Nice to meet you Kevin—ahh—Lace.

FRANKIE
And finally, we have Deb. She's an agnostic. That means, she doesn't know if there's a God; but we're working on her.

(Under a stylish apple jack hat, stands a blonde nineteen year old girl, wearing no make up nor jewelry. A rust colored sheer top displays her leopard spotted bra and busty figure. Her top is short enough to reveal her naval ring and the fact that she is more than a few months pregnant. Six inches of skin separate her piercing from her tightly fitted low-rise jeans.)

HOLLY
(Whispering in Joy's ear)
That's obviously how she got into trouble in the first place.

(Joy nudges Holly again)

DEBBIE
Hey girls.

SAMANTHA
Aren't those jeans a bit restricting in your condition?

DEBBIE
I don't plan on keeping it.

SAMANTHA
(Shocked)
Oh!

JOY
Her.

DEBBIE
Excuse me?

JOY
Your baby, you're going to give birth to a person, not an *it*. So you'll need a lot of support when she's born.

DEBBIE
(Touching her stomach)
How do you know it—ah, I mean *she*, is a girl?

FRANKIE
When *she* decides to get rid of *it*, *we* her friends will be there to support her. But enough of that, the four of us were just discussing the inaccuracy of the Bible. Care to join us?

(Debbie reaches into her low-rise jeans and pulls out a crushed pack of cigarettes and offers one to Joy.)

DEBBIE
Smoke?

FRANKIE
(sarcastically)
She won't take it.

SAMANTHA
I don't see you smoking.

FRANKIE
No. It's bad for your health. But Joy won't take it because she's a Christian.

JOY
I'll smoke if I want to.

HOLLY
Joy!

FRANKIE
Will you now?

(Joy places her book bag on the ground, takes her Bible out, and holds it in her arms next to her chest.)

JOY
So answer me. None of you believe in the Bible?

FRANKIE
None of them believe in organized religion.

JOY
I wasn't talking to you.

FRANKIE
You asked for an answer. You didn't say from whom.

JOY
It doesn't matter. Like I said, I have *your* answer, Frankie. *Job 23:10.*

FRANKIE
What?

JOY
Last time you asked me why God didn't protect me from the soda that was thrown at me. The answer is Job 23:10. "When He is at work in the earth, I do not see him, nor can I catch a glimpse. But He *is* there, and he knows the way that I take."

SAMANTHA
Let's go, Joy. You don't have to do this.

JOY
No. I'm fine. And yes, I do.

(Frankie quickly goes on the attack.)

FRANKIE
You girls seem tense. Maybe you're not getting enough romance in your life, if you know what I mean. You ever think about dating an atheist?

(Joy's eyes follow the group as they laugh.)

JOY
The Bible says, "How can two walk together unless they agree. *Amos 3:3"*

FRANKIE
You've memorized a lot of Scripture from a book you know nothing about.

JOY
The Bible was written by holy men inspired by God.

KEVIN
That's not what we were taught.

RICH
Yeah, it's all a bunch of B.S. anyway.

JOY
Well, maybe what you're being taught is a bunch of B.S.

SAMANTHA
Joy!

FRANKIE
Wanna bet? I can prove to you right now that book was not inspired.

HOLLY
(pulling on Joy)
Joy. Let's go.

JOY
I said I'm fine.

FRANKIE
If I can't, then no more Jesus jokes. I will stay quiet for the rest of the semester.

JOY
Go ahead then, prove it.

FRANKIE
(pointing to himself)
But if I do, then this atheist gets a kiss.

SAMANTHA
No way!

FRANKIE
You scared?

JOY
I'm not scared. Prove it.

FRANKIE
You ever heard of the Documentary Hypothesis?

JOY
No.

FRANKIE
It's a theory that suggests Moses did not write the Pentateuch, but instead it was the calculated work of four different authors.

JOY
That's a lie.

FRANKIE
It was put forth by a German named Julius Wellhausen.

KEVIN
Yeah. He was one of your biblical scholars.

(Joy turns quickly to look at Kevin.)

JOY
Well, it's still only a theory; you haven't proved anything.

FRANKIE
Oh yeah? In Genesis chapter 1, what was the last thing God created?

JOY
Man.

FRANKIE
Then why in Genesis chapter 2 does it say—and I quote—The Lord God had not created fields *nor* plants but first created man—end quote.

(Joy's eyes open wide and her Bible slips from between her arms and hits the ground.)

Frankie
The reason is, two different stories…two different authors.

(Joy looks down at her Bible on the floor.)

(Holly picks up the Bible and hits Frankie with it.)

HOLLY
Jerk!

(Joy turns and begins to walks away.)

FRANKIE
Not so fast. Where's my kiss?

JOY
(looking back)
Kiss him, Kevin.

FRANKIE
Hey! *You* lost the bet.

JOY
You asked for a kiss. You didn't say from whom.

(Joy's walk turns into a sprint. Behind her, Samantha and Holly gather Joy's things and call out to their friend. Joy ignores their calls but instead begins to run cross campus and disappears into the crowd. Her heart races as she makes her way quickly up the steps of the library, into the building, and pass the receptionist who asks her for ID. Joy stops in the building's atrium and franticly looks for the library computers. After finding a free station, she rushes over and quickly types in the words D-O-C-U-M-E-N-T-A-R-Y-H-Y-P-O-T-H-E-S-I-S. She places her hand on her chest and tries to catch her breath, then arbitrarily clicks on one of the many entries and begins to read.)

JOY
Documentary Hypothesis . . . different writing styles suggests Moses did not write . . .

(Joy's eyes glance down the page.)

JOY
. . . Two creations stories proof of different authorship.

(Joy exits out of the site and types in B-I-B-L-E-G-A-T-E-W-A-Y-.-C-O-M...G-E-N-E-S-I-S -C-H-A-P-T-E-R-1 and begins to read.)

JOY
And the earth brought forth grass, and herb yielding seed . . . And the evening and the morning were the third day.

(Joy quickly scrolls down the page and reads.)

JOY
And God created man in his own image . . . and the evening and the morning were the sixth day.

(Having found the text she quoted to Frankie, Joy now frantically types in G-E-N-E-S-I-S -C-H-A-P-T-E-R-2 and begins to read.)

JOY
No shrub of the field had yet appeared on the earth . . . the Lord God formed the man out of the dust . . .

(Joy backs away from the computer.)

JOY
No.

(Frankie's voice again enters Joy's mind and his words play over in her head.)

"Two different stories...two different authors."

(Joy lifts up her eyes in despair.)

FADE TO BLACK

INT. CLASSROOM: IMMEDIATELY AFTER

(Joy is sitting in class and Professor Byrnes is lecturing. She nervously looks around the class and then down at her desk. Carved into the wooden surface are the words, "Help my unbelief." She looks at the little alabaster cross in her left hand and squeezes it tightly with both hands, drawing it close to her heart.)

PROFESSOR BYRNES
In many ancient cultures, the concept of god is strictly a human construct.

STUDENT 3
Man made god?

PROFESSOR BYRNES
Correct. And this human construct takes on different forms as we move from culture to culture. Take for instance the Persian god Mithra. Shepherds were said to be present at his virgin birth. Who does this sound like?

STUDENT 3
Jesus?

(Joy presses her hands against her ears.)

PROFESSOR BYRNES
Precisely. And what about the Egyptian God Horus? He enjoyed
the title "son of god" and was even said to have been resurrected.
Who does this also sound like?

PAUL
Let me guess. Jesus? You know, Professor, you need to study logic.
There are rules of inference that allow us to draw the proper con-
clusion from two pieces of data.

STUDENT 4
What?

PAUL
He's manipulating you! He's presenting information that you're not
familiar with in a way that implies Jesus is a fictional character.

STUDENT 4
What?

PAUL
Mithra was born out of a rock, not a woman; so unless "*rock*" is a
metaphor for his mother having a heart of stone, there goes your
virgin story. And the accounts of shepherds at his birth date back to
the second century A.D. Oh, excuse me, *C.E.* This tells us that *they*
were influenced by Christianity, not the other way around.

PROFESSOR BYRNES
Does it scare you, Mr. Agard that *your* God may not exist? That the
concept of God is in fact a human construct?

PAUL
No, teachers like you scare me because you have no respect for the *subject* of God.

PROFESSOR BYRNES
As a historian, how can I have respect for history's greatest phantom?

(Frankie grins.)

PAUL
A phantom? God is a phantom?

STUDENT 2
So, Professor, you're saying God is not in history? What about all these crazy religions and their practices we've been reading about?

PROFESSOR BYRNES
God is not in history, but the concept of God is, and therefore the belief in deities. And in this context he becomes history's greatest phantom; taking on new forms and identities as he moves from religion to religion; each culture reshaping him into their own image and to suit their own needs. For example, look at the Egyptian gods. They are in the likeness of Egyptians and their animals. The same applies to the Hindu gods.

STUDENT 2
And they even wore Hindu clothing.

PROFESSOR BYRNES
Correct. And each culture borrowed from the next as they interacted, creating hybrid gods and religions. And people like Mr. Agard, who take the Bible literally, are skeptical of science because it reduces their beliefs to nothing more than a security blanket.

(Joy moves her hand across the words on her desk.)
PAUL
Are you teaching us in this class that God does not exist?

PROFESSOR BYRNES
Again, science does not support the existence of God, nor is there any evidence for him whatsoever in history. So you draw your own conclusion.

BLAM!

(Joy's two friends enter the class. Samantha rushes straight to Joy while Holly speaks to the professor.)

HOLLY
Ah—sorry sir. We're here for Joy. She forgot her bag outside.

SAMANTHA
Are you ok?

JOY
Yes, I told you I'm fine.

SAMANTHA
(Wiping Joy's face)
No you're not. Look at you, you're sweating.

(Samantha puts Joy's bag on the floor beside her chair and slams her medication on the desk.)

SAMANTHA
Here's your medication. Take it and we will be back to get you after class.

PROFESSOR BYRNES
Ladies, either take a seat or take your leave.

(The girls pass Frankie as they leave. Samantha reaches out and hits him.)

SAMANTHA
Jerk!

PROFESSOR BYRNES
Ladies!

HOLLY
We're sorry Professor—Ah?

PROFESSOR BYRNES
Byrnes.

HOLLY
Oh, you will.

PROFESSOR BYRNES
Excuse me?

SAMANTHA
She didn't mean anything. C'mon Holly, let's go.

(Frankie laughs and looks at Joy as her friends leave the class.)

(Outside in the hall, Holly and Samantha call Joy's mother.)

CUT TO:
MRS. HUNTER IN KITCHEN

MRS. HUNTER
(on phone)
Is everything all right?

SAMANTHA
Yes, Mrs. Hunter. We found her. She's okay. She's in class.

MRS. HUNTER
Thank God. And thank you, Samantha. Joy's really blessed to have you girls as friends.

(Mrs. Hunter hangs up the phone and walks upstairs to Joy's room. She opens the door slowly and pauses for a moment in the doorway as if remembering something familiar.)

MRS. HUNTER
I'm losing her, Lord.

(Mrs. Hunter enters and stares at the furnishings in her daughter's room. She turns to the night stand by Joy's bed and at the foot of the statuette of Christ is Joy's diary. Mrs. Hunter picks it up and reads the last entry.)

MRS. HUNTER
(Reading)
"Dear Lord, you have done so much for me, but I'm afraid I haven't been a very good child. There have been so many negative thoughts running through my mind lately. But don't worry, God, I'm going to try to be strong. I will not doubt. I will not be ashamed. I will not be silent. I apologize for failing you. It won't happen again."

(Joy's mother looks up to heaven.)

MRS. HUNTER
I trust you Lord; but I don't know how much more she can bear.

(Mrs. Hunter closes the diary, places it back on the nightstand, and walks out.)

CUT TO:
CLASSROOM

(Joy sits at her desk staring at her medication.)

FRANKIE
So Professor, if God does not exist, then where did we come from?

PROFESSOR BYRNES
Science has answers for that Frankie. Evolution says that—

PAUL
(Turning to Frankie)
You are a monkey.

FRANKIE
What did you call me?

PROFESSOR BYRNES
Mr. Agard, you are out of line!

PAUL
Are you offended, Professor?

PROFESSOR BYRNES
Yes, in fact I am! It is offensive to me to hear you call another
human being a monkey. You have no right to do so.

PAUL
Well, then think about how I must feel when you sit up there and
teach me that I come from one.

*(The two men stare at each other; Paul waits for the professor's
next move.)*

PROFESSOR BYRNES
So evolution scares you, Mr. Agard? Well, it should. Because it is
the scientific big brother that tells the church it's time to put away
its security blanket.

PAUL
And what about you, Professor? Are you afraid to believe? Or is it
my faith that scares you, because in your heart you want to believe
but just can't. The fact is it takes more faith to believe in evolution
than it does to believe in God. Evolution is not monkeys attempting to become man, it's man attempting to become monkeys.

(The class laughs.)

PROFESSOR BYRNES
Again, Mr. Agard, I would prefer the facts in this class, something that you have yet to give, and not your coy remarks. And I have news for you, or if you would prefer, a revelation. Evolution is no longer a theory, it is a proven fact.

PAUL
(Paul turns to the class.)
Is that so? I bet most of you don't even know what evolution is.

PAUL (CONT'D)
(looking at student 2)
Do you?

STUDENT 2
No.

PAUL
But you believe in it?

STUDENT 2
Yes. They wouldn't teach it to us if it wasn't true. Isn't that right professor?

(All eyes turn to Professor Byrnes.)

PROF. BYRNES
Hmm. Evolution is...

PAUL
Well, Professor?

PROF. BYRNES
Change with modification within a given organism over long periods of time. And to support the fact that men have evolved from apes, scientists have in captivity a gorilla named Koko, who has learned to speak.

STUDENT 1
Get out of here, Professor. Is that true?

PROFESSOR BYRNES
Yes it is. You can look it up for yourself at Koko.org.

STUDENT 1
She has her own Web site?

(The class laughs.)

PAUL
This is ridiculous. And just how long will it take for Koko to
become a human?

STUDENT 2
He said it takes millions of years. You're not listening.

PAUL
You know what, why don't you check back with Koko in a million
years?

STUDENT 2
Exactly...Wait, Hey—

PAUL
We see mutations in animals all the time. Scientists even have a fly
with an extra pair of wings. But none of these mutations are in
favor of macroevolution. They usually end in diseases and work
against the animal's survival.

FRANKIE
Well, a mutation in an ape named Lucy made her bipedal and eventually human. In Laetoli, they even found 3.5 million years old
footprints of these apes walking upright. Since this class began,
I've been doing my research.

(Frankie looks over at Joy and smiles.)

PAUL
Oh yeah? Well the scientist that found the footprints as well as the expert that analyzed them said they were human. I did my research before entering this class.

FRANKIE
It doesn't make a difference. They're in the textbooks as belonging to apes, and it's proof of evolution by way of mutation.

STUDENT 5
Mutations do not work like that. Even if you had a mutation that caused an animal to walk upright, it doesn't mandate subsequent mutations that would turn it or its offspring into a man.

FRANKIE
And how do you know? Who the heck are you?

STUDENT 5
Juan Herrera, biology major. Pre-med, Amigo.

PAUL
My man! Thank you, Mr. Herrera. And there are *more* flaws in the evolutionary theory, such as the lack of transitional forms in the fossil record?

FRANKIE
Science has found a number of fossils they believe to be transitional.

PROFESSOR BYRNES
Thank *you* Mr. Johnson, the best case being the whale, in which they have found three probable intermediate—

(Paul interrupts)

PAUL
Three? Three probable intermediate forms?

(Paul leaves his seat and heads toward the blackboard. As he passes the professor's desk, he notices a book entitled, "The Illusion of God." Within the pages, the photograph of Prof. Byrnes' daughter sticks out like a bookmark. Paul picks up a piece of chalk and writes an equation across the breadth of the board.)

PROFESSOR BYRNES
(angrily)
Mr. Agard!

PAUL
(Pointing to the board)
There is anywhere from 10-100 million species of animals in the world today, and according to evolutionists, each having evolved over millions of years. If each species had just two transitional forms and your best case is three *probable* intermediate forms between a hyena like creature and a whale? If macroevolution has happened, there should be countless transitional forms, but instead the fossil records are silent.

(Joy notices the frustration of the girl sitting next to her.)

GIRL
That guy's an idiot.

STUDENT 3
If not evolution, then how do you explain the existence of life?

PAUL
(looking at the professor)
Intelligent design.

(Paul walks back to his seat and slams the chalk on top of the professor's book.)

PROFESSOR BYRNES
Mr. Agard, I have a problem with Christians pushing intelligent design on us which is just another form of refried creation myths. In science, everything must be falsifiable, The myths of the Bible

are not. And right at the foot of this desk is an invisible line. Do not cross it again.

(Frankie taps the student next to him.)

FRANKIE
One day I'm gonna show that religious nut just how crazy he is.

PAUL
Well, in an attempt to remove its discrepancies, the theory of evolution has *evolved*.

FRANKIE
What the hell are you talking about?

PAUL
The discovery of DNA has changed everything. Originally, evolutionists believed in "Inheritance of acquired characteristics." They thought animals adapted to their environment and those adaptive traits were passed on to their offspring. But this was proven wrong. Next up was *Darwin's* "Natural selection" as *the* mechanism of evolution; but this was also not accurate. Today, hereditary or germline mutations in the sex cells of the parents are said to be the primary mechanism of evolution in which Natural selection acts upon.

STUDENT 3
I don't get it. DNA is still within the animal, right? So if the animal adapts—

JUAN
DNA doesn't adapt, it replicates, by a very specific process.

PAUL
Yes, that which the parent was, the child shall be. Monkey begets monkey and man begets man. Just like the Bible says.

PROFESSOR BYRNES
Well, pardon the expression, "thank god," we are not confined to religion for our answers. Today we stress evolution in our educational system even on a high school level, and not creation.

PAUL

Wrong again! We stress evolution in our classrooms because of the Cold War. 1957. The Soviets launched Sputnik and America got nervous. We felt we were falling behind in the area of science. So our government funded the National Science Foundation, which came up with a secular curriculum to be taught in public schools. Enter evolution. It made its way into the textbooks because of political competition, not because it was scientifically true.

FRANKIE

Is that true, Professor?

PAUL

And in 1987, the Supreme Court to deem teaching creation unconstitutional, and it was removed from the classroom. Christian parents and students never had a chance. The monkey had won.

PROFESSOR BYRNES

Well, it would seem the monkey has gotten the best of you.

(The class laughs.)

PAUL

Then let's have an open debate. Student vs. Professor. Man vs. Monkey. You represent Koko the gorilla and evolution, and I will represent God and intelligent design.

(Professor Byrnes looks at the chalk Paul placed on his book. He runs his hand across the edge of the photograph between the pages.)

PROFESSOR BYRNES

Maybe when you get a PhD and your own class, will I consider having an open debate with you, until then, I am the teacher and this is my class, and you are just a student working toward your Associates. But I do have a question for you, one that has troubled historians and philosophers alike.

PAUL

And what is it?

PROFESSOR BYRNES
Throughout history there has been one constant. *"Suffering."*

(From a forgotten corner in the class, Joy raises her head.)

PAUL
And?

PROFESSOR BYRNES
But Christianity claims, that the God who created this world and sustains it, is all-knowing, all powerful, and perfectly good. If each of these claims are true, then it is difficult to understand why the God of your Bible allows suffering to persist. Thus, the existence of suffering is conclusive evidence that at least one of these central claims of Christianity is false. Or quite possibly, Mr. Agard, God does not exist.

(Joy reaches for the medication bottle.)

STUDENT 1
I don't understand, Professor. What do you mean?

PROFESSOR BYRNES
It is the age-old question of man, *"The problem of suffering."*
One, If God exists then he is omniscient, omnipotent, and perfectly good.

JOY
(whispering to herself)
Yes.

PROFESSOR BYRNES
Two, if God were omniscient, omnipotent, and perfectly good, then the world would contain no suffering.

JOY
(whispering hopefully)
Yes.

PROFESSOR BYRNES
Three, the world contains suffering.

(Joy runs her finger across the label on her medication.)

JOY
(whispering sadly)
Yes.

PROFESSOR
Conclusion, therefore God does not exist!

JOY
(whispering in despair)
Yes...

(Joy's treasured memories of her Christian life flash before her eyes as if they were files being wiped clean. In her mind she screams.)

(Joy collects her things and hurries for the classroom door. In her haste, she trips over one of the student's desks and hits the ground; her medication bottle and the contents of her bag lay exposed on the floor. She fights to hold back the tears. While Paul, obsessed with getting his point across to the professor, does not even notice Joy has fallen behind him.)

SHOT: (SLOW MOTION)
CAMERA SHOWS JOY GATHERING HER THINGS ON THE FLOOR AS PAUL SPEAKS.

PAUL
The problem, Professor, is that you are a subjective creature trying to understand a transcendent God. You are the limited, grasping at

the limitless. At best, your conclusions will end in error. At worst, your conclusions will end in despair.

(With belongings in her hand, Joy heads for the exit.)

INT. HALLWAY/COLLEGE BATHROOM - IMMEDIATELY AFTER.
(Joy runs out the class, through the halls, and into the bathroom. She drops her books and collapses in a corner against the stall. She curses the medication in her right hand and throws the bottle across the room. The orange cylinder hits the wall and opens. The little pills spread out across the floor and make their way back to Joy. She opens her left hand and stares at the cross in her palm. Her mind begins to drifts back to the night she received the little cross.)

FLASHBACK MEMORY. THE HUNTER'S HOUSE-JOY'S BEDROOM – NIGHT
(A five-year-old Joy struggles with the fear of dying and the pain of her sickness.)

LITTLE JOY
Mommy.

MRS. HUNTER
Yes, Joy?

LITTLE JOY
I'm afraid.

MRS. HUNTER
Of what, baby?

LITTLE JOY
Why am I always in so much pain? Am I going to die?

MRS. HUNTER
No, baby. You're just a little sick, and sometimes when people are sick, they suffer with a little pain.

LITTLE JOY
Why do people have to suffer? And what will happen to me if I *do* die?

MRS. HUNTER
(Tears form in her eyes)
I don't know why people suffer baby, but you will not die tonight.

LITTLE JOY
I'm scared.

MRS. HUNTER
You don't have to be baby. You know why?

LITTLE JOY
Why?

MRS. HUNTER
(wiping the tears from her own face.)
Because you are God's little girl. And the Bible says that God loved you so much that he sent his son Jesus to die for you. But death was not strong enough to hold Jesus in the grave. And as long as Jesus lives, suffering and death have no power over you either. So you don't have to be afraid my love, all you have to do is believe.

LITTLE JOY
Mommy.

MRS. HUNTER
Yes, Joy?

LITTLE JOY
I'm still afraid.

MRS. HUNTER
That's all right. God's watching over you. He'll keep you safe.
(Mrs. Hunter takes a statuette of the cross from Joy's dresser and sets it on her daughter's nightstand.)

(Joy stares at the statuette.)

LITTLE JOY
But I'm tired. Doesn't God get tired too?

MRS. HUNTER
No, baby. He neither slumbers nor sleeps.

(Mrs. Hunter removes a small golden crucifix edged in alabaster from around her neck and hangs it on the statuette. She kisses her daughter good night and turns out the light. After her mother leaves the room, Joy gets out of bed, turns on the light, and stares at the small white trinket. She takes it from off its place on the cross and places it around her own neck. The golden chain moves over her head and down her hair. The beautiful alabaster edged cross comes to rest softly on her chest, above her heart. She kneels at her bedside, closes her eyes and says a silent prayer. When she is done, she opens her eyes and utters two words audibly.)

LITTLE JOY
I believe.

(Joy gets back in bed.)

LITTLE JOY (CONT'D)
(Looking up to heaven)
I'm going to sleep now. Please don't forget to watch over me. Oh yeah, and thank you, Jesus. I'm no longer afraid.

(Joy turns out the light.)

(Outside, Mrs. Hunter stops by the stairs and turns on the hallway light. Worried about Joy, she turns and heads back to her daughter's room. She opens the door and the light from the hallway bursts into Joy's room and strikes the statuette, producing an image of the cross on the wall over Joy's bed. Mrs. Hunter leans in the doorway and begins to cry.)

CUT TO:
SCHOOL BATHROOM

(Back in the college bathroom, Joy is curled up on the floor crying. She closes her hand and clutching the cross she received as a child.)

JOY
My heart says you're *real*, God, but in my mind I keep hearing—

"God does not exist"

EXT. BUS STOP: IMMEDIATELY AFTER
(Joy decides to go to the mall to clear her head. As she stands at the bus stop, she spies her homeless friend across the street, but this time she withdraws from his view. For the first time in her life she begins to see the world differently. As Joy boards the bus, the narrator begins to speak.)

PROFESSOR BYRNES (NARRATOR)
Each time a teacher meets with his student, he attempts to make that child see the world differently, through *his* eyes. It is truly a subconscious effort, I assure you; and most teachers will deny this. But that a teacher imprints his or her views on a student is a truth nonetheless. *"The world is filled with war, death, and cruelty, and history proves it."* This or some similar thesis statement I always gave to my students as an introduction on the first day of my history class. Not because it's how I viewed history, but because it's how I viewed the world. Look at the world now, Joy. Do you see it?

(Joy takes a window seat and sees a man and his son being charitable to her homeless friend.)

PROFESSOR (NARRATOR) (CONT'D)
Look closer; beyond kindness.

(She watches as the man and his son move on.)

PROFESSOR (NARRATOR) (CONT'D)
Look, you will see it, in his eyes.

(Joy looks at the homeless man sitting there all alone.)

PROFESSOR BYRNES (NARRATOR) (CONT'D)
There it is. Despair.

(Joy weeps silently.)

FADE IN:
MALL

(Joy sits at the food court in the mall where she and her friends were a few weeks earlier. A young couple walks by her, laughing and cuddling.)

PROFESSOR (NARRATOR) (CONT'D)
Don't turn away. Look, beyond happiness, beyond love.

(As the couple passes her, Joy sees the elderly woman she and her friends ministered to also sitting alone.)

PROFESSOR (NARRATOR) (CONT'D)
Look and you will see it, just as I saw it; *neglect*. Someone has forgotten. How can there be a God?

(On her way home, Joy sits on the bus. A dismal look crosses her face as she stares out the window at her new world.)

PROFESSOR (NARRATOR) (CONT'D)
You never saw the world this way before. But I didn't change the world. I just changed how you saw it. It is within the power of an educator to change the way a student views the world, but it is not his charge.

INT. TEACHERS LOUNGE. - AFTERNOON

(After his bout with Paul, Professor Byrnes storms into the teacher's lounge where two of his colleagues are sitting, and vents his frustration about the outspoken student.)

PROFESSOR BYRNES
That pompous, arrogant pup.

PROF. HANK
Who are you talking about?

PROFESSOR BYRNES
The apostle Paul. Who else?

PROF. HANK
The apostle Paul?

PROFESSOR BYRNES
A student in my class, his name is Paul. The nerve of him; he had the audacity to challenge *me*, a university professor, to a debate on evolution verses intelligent design. The nerve of him.

PROF. DEAN
I'd like a crack at him.

PROF. HANK
Jim, don't you teach ancient history?

PROFESSOR BYRNES
(Answering sarcastically)
Yes, Hank, I do.

PROF. HANK
So where did evolution come from?

(Professor Byrnes looks coyly at Hank.)

PROF. HANK (CONT'D)
Jim, I warned you about that before. If you have an issue with God and Christianity, the classroom is not the place for it.

PROFESSOR BYRNES
Oh come on, Hank. I don't need more of your Christian babble.

PROF. DEAN
No, by all means, Jim, let the Christian babble.

(Prof. Hank looks over angrily at Dean.)

PROF. DEAN (CONT'D)
Sounds like you had an eventful day; what else happened?

PROFESSOR BYRNES
Some girl got up and ran out the class.

PROF. HANK
For what reason?

PROFESSOR BYRNES
How am I supposed to know? She's not my kid. I'm not responsible for them outside my class. Whatever happened, her parents will have to deal with it when she gets home.

PROF. DEAN
No need for worry, Jim. The latest polls say that 25 percent of all college graduates reject the Bible as the word of God.

(Prof. Dean looks at Prof. Hank)

PROF. DEAN (CONT'D)
And the numbers are rising.

PROF. HANK
What are you getting at?

PROF. DEAN
Look around this campus. By the end of the school year, one out of every four students you see will no longer be controlled by your God.

INT. JOY'S HOUSE - EVENING

(Joy's parents are in the kitchen, waiting for her to come home.)

MR. HUNTER
Baby, it's getting late. Where in the world is Joy?

MRS. HUNTER
She had that history class today, Dwayne. You know; the one with that professor.

MR. HUNTER
I've been meaning to call the school about that man. If he doesn't stop pressuring Joy, he and I are going to have some real problems.

MRS. HUNTER
God would never let our little girl lose faith. We've just got to trust her and pray she'll be strong. She's in college now and she's his student. Besides, he's a professor. He's got to see how this class is affecting her.

MR. HUNTER
Yes, but she was my daughter before she was his student. He may not see the effects of this class, but I do. It's me who she comes home to every night. And it's me who she's stopped praying with.

MRS. HUNTER
I know. Every Monday I'm in prayer, not knowing what state my daughter will be in when she walks through that door.

BLAM!

(Joy's parents walk into the next room.)

MRS. HUNTER (CONT'D)
Joy?

(An angry Joy stops, but does not look at her parents.)

MRS. HUNTER (CONT'D)
Joy, what's wrong?

JOY
Nothing.

MRS. HUNTER
(Attempting to put her arm around Joy)
Baby, what's wrong?

JOY
(Shrugging her mother away)
Not now, Mom. I don't want to talk.

MR. HUNTER
What? You don't want to talk?

JOY
No, Daddy. Please, I just want to go to my room.

MR. HUNTER
It's that class, isn't it? And that damn professor. I knew it. You never should have—

JOY
What!? Never should have what!? Lived this long!? Went to college!? Taken history!? Ask you questions that you couldn't answer!? You know what, I am going upstairs.

(Joy pushes past her parents and attempts to go upstairs)

MR. HUNTER
Joy, stop!

(Mr. Hunter grabs Joy by the arm.)

JOY
(Screaming)
What!

MR. HUNTER
What's gotten into you?

JOY
The truth!

MR. HUNTER
What truth!? Whose truth!?

JOY
The world's truth! The truth that they teach in textbooks! The truth
that they teach in schools! The truth about the Bible, God, Jesus!

MR. HUNTER
And what truth is that? What could they possibly teach you about
Jesus?

JOY
(screaming)
That he doesn't exist!

*(Joy's father is shocked by words he never thought would be spoken
in his home. Without thinking, he reacts.)*

Smack!

(Joy holds her cheek surprised that her father struck her.)

MR. HUNTER (CONT'D)
(shouting)
Not in my house! Not in my house!

MRS. HUNTER
I'm calling the pastor.

JOY
No! Don't call him!

(Joy's mother begins to cry.)

JOY (CONT'D)
(crying)
I'm sorry, Dad. But you don't understand. I feel like I have been
living a lie that you and Mom have perpetuated. All my life I've
suffered, but I have always believed in a God that was bigger than

my pain. That watched over me. So even if I didn't understand why I was sick, I *knew* that God loved me, that my life somehow still had meaning, a purpose. But today, I learned that he doesn't exist.

(Mr. Hunter holds Joy close to his chest.)

JOY (CONT'D)
Today, I learned, Daddy, that he's a phantom—

(Joy pushes away from her father.)

JOY (CONT'D)
And I've put my trust in something that was never there! Do you know what that means? Do you have an answer for that? Do you have an answer for me?

MR. HUNTER
Joy—

JOY (CONT'D)
I didn't think so.

(Joy turns and walks up the stairs. Mr. Hunter reaches out to her. He notices that it is with the same hand he struck her with and draws it back.)

(Joy walks straight over to her bed, kneels, and begins to pray.)

JOY
Answer me. Please. I really need you, God. There're so many thoughts running through my head and I really need you to answer me. Pleeease God, please. If you are real... If you are there.

(Joy waits for a response but her calls are answered with silence.)

JOY (CONT'D)
I've always loved you, God. I have always believed. But now, I don't know. I'm scared again. But God, if you answer me tonight, I promise you, I'll never doubt again.

(Joy waits again for a reply but hears nothing.)

JOY (CONT'D)
You don't exist, that's why you won't answer me. You don't exist!

(Angry, Joy gets up from the floor and begins to look around. The Christian items that decorate her room now become a source of frustration. She moves towards her dresser and with her right arm; violently sweep the gospel CDs, tracts, and Bibles off the counter and on to the floor. She rushes to the walls and rips the pictures from their place. She stops only to scream.)

JOY (CONT'D)
Why won't you answer me?

(Joy grabs one of the framed pictures that read "Jesus the Good Shepherd" and flings it across the room.)

SMASH!

(Joy turns toward her dresser and looks at her self in the shattered mirror. Behind her broken image, she can see her room in disarray; it is a reflection of her troubled soul.)

(She falls to her knees.)

JOY (CONT'D)
God, what will happen to me now?

(Joy falls asleep at the foot of her bed. The only unmoved object in her room is the cross on her nightstand. The previous commotion has moved the mouse connected to her PC, awakening the computer from sleep mode. A video screen saver flashes different pictures and messages. As the music begins to play softly, the light

from the monitor reaches into the room as if beckoning to Joy. At the bottom, the Web address scrolls across the screen. http://www.wisehearts.com/yaam.html)

INT. CLASS ROOM: DAY

(Joy is in class one week later and she sees Professor Byrnes in a new light. Not as a man to be afraid of, but as someone who has the answers to her questions.)

PROFESSOR BYRNES
We are now entering the stage of our course where we will be discussing Greece and its culture. The Greeks are significant in history for a number of reasons. One of which is that they sought to define the world *without* the existence of God.

(Joy draws a cross in her book and writes the words," Why won't you answer me?" "Why?" She then scratches it out.)

PROFESSOR BYRNES (CONT'D)
As you know, there *were* Gods in the Greek culture, but there came a point when they stopped viewing the world through the eyes of a deity that they could not see, and started viewing it through the eyes of man.

(Joy looks up attentively at the professor.)

PROFESSOR BYRNES (CONT'D)
For example, the Greek poet Homer, 850 B.C.E, in the opening address to the Iliad, invites a goddess to relate the story. But the Greek historian Herodotus, fifth century B.C.E, does not. When he writes of historical conflicts, he documents what man did, as seen by a man. He does not need divine aid. Think about it for one second, a world without God. So when men went to war, was it because God wills it, as the Christian church declared when the crusaders massacred the Jews and the Muslims in Jerusalem? Or was it because these were cruel, barbarous men, who were driven by prejudice, greed, and religious zeal?

PAUL
Professor—

PROFESSOR BYRNES
Not today, Mr. Agard. I have the floor.

(Paul slumps back in his chair.)

PROFESSOR BYRNES (CONT'D)
And not just history. We owe a lot to the Greeks in the area of math,
science, and philosophy, which allows for learning and teaching
through questioning. Greek philosophers were curious about the
world they lived in, and they dared to do what previous societies
would not. They asked the question *why*.

(Joy looks down at the word written on her paper. "Why?")

PROFESSOR BYRNES (CONT'D)
A key point of interest; what's the consequence of defining the
world without the concept of God?

PAUL
Hell.

*(Joy looks angrily at Paul and then turns to the professor as he
answers.)*

PROFESSOR BYRNES
No, Mr. Agard.

STUDENT 3
What's the consequence, Professor?

PROFESSOR BYRNES
Asking the question, "*why*."

STUDENT 3
What?

PROFESSOR BYRNES
Think about it. You grew up all your life viewing the world through the eyes of a religious machine that claimed it represented God. In such a society there are no questions. There is just obedience to instructions. If you have questions, you must suppress them. And if there are no questions, then there are no answers. But the Greeks began to seek answers. For example, in medicine, if you remove the concept of God, you must ask the question, *"Why do people get sick?"*

(Joy looks at the medicine in her bag.)

PROFESSOR BYRNES (CONT'D)
The Greeks were some of the first people to look at the cause of sickness and treat diseases medically. Before this, disease was mostly treated by superstitious methods, because they thought the cause was related to some wrong action committed by the individual toward the gods. And one thing I would like for all of you to get from this course is for you to ask questions. You are the leaders of tomorrow. If you are to get the answers to the questions that plague man, you must remove the obstacles in your life that keep you from asking the question *why.* And in some ancient cultures that obstacle was God.

(Professor Byrnes looks at the clock and sees the class has ended.)

PROFESSOR BYRNES (CONT'D)
That's all the time we have for today. Don't forget to study for the exam next week.

(As the students leave, the professor turns to erase the board. Joy remains behind, looking down at her book and the question on the paper. "Why?")

(Joy walks over to the professor.)

JOY
Professor?

PROFESSOR BYRNES
(turning around)
Oh, yes, Joy?

JOY
I've had a lot of questions lately and—

PROFESSOR BYRNES
Ms. Hunter, we educators encourage our students to come to us when they need help. My office hours are Tuesdays from one to five.

(Joy drops her head and Professor Byrnes realizes that she's troubled.)

PROFESSOR BYRNES (CONT'D)
But, as it were, my next class has a film assignment in which they are to write a report. So I'm actually free this period to answer your questions. Those of faith would say this is divine ordination.

(Joy smiles.)

JOY
That's what I wanted to talk to you about, Professor.

PROFESSOR BYRNES
What's that?

JOY
My faith.

PROFESSOR BYRNES
(grinning smugly)
And what about your faith?

JOY
Well . . . I feel so awkward.

(Professor Byrnes notices Joy squeezing something in her hand.)

PROFESSOR
It's okay, Joy. Don't be afraid. Just say it.

(Joy struggles to speak. But instead puts her hand over her face to hide the tears.)

PROFESSOR BYRNES
(Reaching for Joy's shoulder)
It's OK Miss Hunter. Tell me what's wrong.

(Embarrassed, Joy leans into the professor. Her head rests on his chest.)

PROFESSOR BYRNES
Uhh . . . Ms. Hunter?

JOY
(Crying)
I have questions, thoughts... doubts. Questions about Jesus, the Bible, and... suffering. If He's real...why do we suffer?

(The professor is caught off guard by Joy's actions. But the young girl's touch seems to awaken something tragic within him. A look of sorrow crosses his face.)

PROFESSOR BYRNES
Yes child, why?

JOY
(Looking up at Professor Byrnes)
I have questions . . . but no answers.

(The professor's arms close around Joy.)

PROFESSOR BYRNES
It's all right, child. We'll help you get the answers to your questions. I promise you.

INT. CAMPUS CAFE - IMMEDIATELY AFTER.

(The professor brings Joy a cup of tea and some tissues.)

PROFESSOR BYRNES
Here you are, my dear, a tissue for your tears and a cup of tea to warm your spirit.

JOY
I'm sorry, Professor. I'm so embarrassed. I didn't mean to—

PROFESSOR BYRNES
Nonsense, child. Contrary to Mr. Agard's assessment of me, I am quite human, you know.

JOY
I just didn't know where else to turn. It's like since I've taken this class, I don't know…my mind, my thoughts.

(The professor sees Joy still squeezing her cross.)

PROFESSOR BYRNES
The answer is *tea*.

JOY
Tea?

PROFESSOR BYRNES
Yes, *tea*. I have offered you tea to calm your spirit, but you have not yet touched it. You see, Joy, to take hold of what I am offering you— *tea*, you have to put down what you're holding— *your cross*. And your holding on to your religious beliefs is stopping you from getting the answers to the questions that are troubling.

(Joy draws her hands away from the professor.)

PROFESSOR BYRNES (CONT'D)
Tell me, Joy, do you know the origin of that trinket?

JOY
(Smiling)
Yes. My mother gave it to me when I was a child. I was sick and scared and that night something special hap— I mean, it's dear to me.

PROFESSOR BYRNES
That's a sweet story I'm sure, but I was actually referring to its historical origin, not its significance to you. Do you know it?

JOY
It's Christian isn't it?

PROFESSOR BYRNES
Not quite. It's Roman, but it has come to be identified with Christianity.

(The professor leans in and opens Joy's hand.)

PROFESSOR BYRNES (CONT'D)
How can something so small be so heavy?

(Joy closes her hand and pulls it near her.)

PROFESSOR BYRNES (CONT'D)
No need to hide it from me.

JOY
It really means a lot to me, Professor.

PROFESSOR BYRNES
I'm sure it does. You see, it's like we discussed in class. Sometimes we put too much significance into a thing. Like religion. It can make you smile, but it comes with a price. It has a hold on you. And one day when life demands that you move on, you find that you can't, because things like this trinket keep pulling you back. Here, I have something for you.

JOY
What is it, Professor?

(The professor takes a book from his bag and places it on the table.)

PROFESSOR BYRNES
It's a book, but don't let the title frighten you. What is important is that the author explains the philosophy of religion, which is the human need to create divine sources of comfort. It helps us make sense of the world. So, we develop a system of religious beliefs, pick a god, and sit him on top of it. Then we take our own virtues and our own prejudices and assign them to stone or metal images like the one you have in your hand, that cross. And it now becomes priceless to us. But in reality it has no value at all.

(Professor Byrnes places the cup of tea on top of the book and slides it over to Joy who hesitates to pick it up.)

PROFESSOR BYRNES (CONT'D)
I know that was a lot for you. Tell me, how do you feel?

JOY
I don't know. Upset.

PROFESSOR BYRNES
Why upset?

JOY
I don't know? Upset at myself for not knowing what I believe; and even for believing. I feel like I did when I was little. Just like you said in class a few weeks ago, I was one of the last kids to stop believing in Santa Claus.

PROFESSOR BYRNES
Do tell.

JOY
My friends used to make fun of me all the time and one Christmas I got so upset that I left a note with the cookies I left for Santa Claus that said, "Dear Santa, please don't touch; these are for the Tooth Fairy."

(A large smile graces the face of Professor Byrnes accompanied by a chuckle.)

JOY (CONT'D)
Professor, you smiled!

PROFESSOR BYRNES
(chuckling)
Yes, Joy, I did. It would seem that you have that effect on me. I don't know if that's good or bad.

JOY
I think it's good, Professor. You have a nice smile.

PROFESSOR BYRNES
(smiling)
The tooth fairy, Joy?

JOY
(smiling)
I know. I was a kid.

(The professor stares at Joy as if there was something familiar about her.)

JOY (CONT'D)
You know, I feel much better now. Thank you, Professor.

PROFESSOR BYRNES
Answers to questions often have that effect on people. But I must admit, *you* have also made *me* feel a little better.

(Joy drops her cross on the table and reaches for the tea. After taking a sip, she reads the title of the book.)

JOY
The Illusion of God, huh?

PROFESSOR BYRNES
Yes, and tomorrow, why don't you meet me here on campus for our next session.

INT. PROFESSOR BYRNES' HOUSE/DEN- LATER THAT EVENING

(Professor Byrnes returns home and goes straight to his computer. He accesses the college Web site and types in "campus art show" and then the word "LIFE." After making a few selections and writing them on a piece of paper, he retires for the evening.)

CUT TO:
PROFESSOR BYRNES' BEDROOM

(As the night progresses, Professor Byrnes lays in bed troubled by a dream.)

DREAM SEQUENCE:

PROFESSOR BYRNES' HOUSE/DAUGHTER'S ROOM.

(A small table stands in a child's room set with toy saucers and teacups. Next to the table Professor Byrnes reads to his daughter from the Bible as she sits on his lap, playfully sipping from her cup. Behind them are a series of medication bottles on his daughter's dresser.)

(Suddenly, Professor Byrnes screams.)

PROFESSOR BYNRES
No!

(The Bible and cup fall to the ground. The tea cup breaks.)

(Suddenly, the paramedics are in the little girl's room fighting to save her life.)

EMT 1
Please sir, You've gotta give us room!

(The Professor struggles to see his daughter but his wife and a friend hold him back.)

FRIEND (PROFESSOR HANK)
Please, Jim, let the attendants do their job. Right now the best thing we can do for her is pray.

EMT 1
Yes. You've got to stand back.

(Professor Byrnes retreats to a corner in his daughter's room and begins to pray.)

PROFESSOR BYNRES
If you can hear me, Lord, grant me this one thing. Let her live, please.

(The heart monitor flat lines.)

Beeeeeeeeeep!

EMT 2
We're losing her!

(Professor Byrnes pushes past his wife and friend only to see the EMT working on his daughter's lifeless body. The EMT's large hands press down over and over on her tiny chest.)

(The dream ends and Professor Byrnes awakes in a sweat and screams.)

PROFESSOR BYRNES
Noooo!

(The professor looks at the clock, which says three a.m. and real-izes it was just a bad dream. He sits up on the side of his bed and looks around the room at the bare walls. He opens the drawer next to his bed which is filled with framed pictures. He takes one out and stares hard at the family in the portrait. In anger he punches it, breaking the glass cover and cutting his hand.)

EXT. SCHOOL CAMPUS ART SHOW- THE NEXT DAY
(The professor takes Joy to an art display on campus for their next session. He plans to use the paintings to address her questions about God and suffering. His hand is wrapped in a bandage as a result of the night before.)

PROFESSOR BYRNES
I have three paintings to show you. Each entitled "*Life.*" They were donated by local agencies in the neighborhood and are part of a project by the schools' art director to show that everyone is capa-ble of telling a story through art. But we will use them to gain some insight into the paradox of God and human suffering.

(Joy looks around at all the different artwork.)

JOY
They're beautiful, Professor. Who painted them?

PROFESSOR BYRNES
This first collection comes from the *Love, Peace, & Joy* Christian day care.

(Seeing the connection with her name, Joy looks at the professor.)

JOY
Love, Peace, and "*Joy,*" Professor?

PROFESSOR BYRNES
Purely coincidental, I assure you.

(Joy smiles.)

PROFESSOR BYRNES (CONT'D)
This is our first painting.

(The professor points to a painting filled with bright colors. Scribbled at the top of the canvas, in no particular format, is the title, "Life.")

PROFESSOR BYRNES (CONT'D)
Take a look at it and tell me what you see.

(Joy looks at the painting of box-figured children playing on what appears to be slides and swings in a park, the sun hanging high and bright in the sky. The picture is drawn on white paper, in bright colors.)

JOY
I think it's wonderful.

PROFESSOR BYRNES
Yes. Life *is* wonderful, if you are a four-year-old child who is not aware of life's cruelties. It would be easy for them to believe in a good and benevolent God. Because to them, life is a playground and every moment is filled with happiness.

JOY
I agree. That's why it's wonderful.

PROFESSOR BYRNES
But as we will see in the next group of paintings, life is not filled with happiness alone; it is also filled with suffering and *in life* we develop coping mechanisms to help us deal with our suffering. Yours is religion.

JOY
And what's your coping mechanism Professor?

PROFESSOR BYRNES
Let's move on.

(The next group of art work they look at is noticeably more detailed and skillfully drawn.)

PROFESSOR BYRNES
This group comes from the "Hands of Hope Foster Home" here in town. These children have learned by experience that *life* is *not* a playground. Some family tragedy has left them all alone, that's why some of their paintings are darker. If they are to move on, they must put away the idea of a benevolent God and accept the truth, that life is filled with tragedy.

(Joy stares at one of the paintings. On a pale gray background is a picture of a young girl with a flower in her hair. She is seated in a chair reading a story to five children sitting on the floor. Four of the children are turned away from the storyteller, each holding a memento from their past and wearing a different expression of hurt on their face. Only the little girl nearest the storyteller is smiling and listening attentively, as she cradles four flowers in her arms.)

PROFESSOR BYRNES (CONT'D)
Tell me, Joy, what do you think about the painting?

JOY
(Still looking at the picture)
That life is filled with tragedy.

(Professor Byrnes shakes his head in affirmation.)

JOY (CONT'D)
But God is aware of it all and plans to address every hurt.

PROFESSOR BYRNES
What? And how pray tell, do you gather all of that from looking at this picture?

(Joy turns to the professor.)

JOY
I know the artist.

(The professor is shocked at Joy's answer.)

(At the bottom of the painting in the lower right-hand corner is the artist's signature. A flower decorating the last letter in her name: "Ahdi.")

JOY (CONT'D)
See the children, they are the victims in life; each one hurt and unable to get past their own pain. Look at their faces. There are four of them, sorrow, fear, loneliness, and anger.

(Professor Byrnes follows Joy's hand to the last child in the picture. The child farthest from the storyteller is an angry little boy looking at a picture of his family. Professor Byrnes looks down at his bandaged hand.)

JOY (CONT'D)
But look at the little girl on the left. See her flowers; they're messages from God to give to the children. And she knows that she is in this place because there is someone she has to help. That's why she's smiling.

(Joy turns to the professor.)

JOY (CONT'D)
What's the next picture?

(Professor Byrnes is still entranced by what Joy has said.)

PROFESSOR BYRNES
Huh?

JOY
You said there were three pictures.

PROFESSOR BYRNES
Oh. Yes, of course. Behind you, over to the left.

(Joy and Professor Byrnes walk over to the last group of pictures, which were obviously drawn by art students. They stop and the professor points to a black canvas layered in thick paints that give form and feel to the figure in the painting. It is a graphic depiction of Christ on the cross. His head is hung low and mourners are gathered at his feet. Just off to the side of Joy and the professor, a tall stranger is also admiring the painting.)

PROFESSOR BYRNES (CONT'D)
What do you think of our last selection?

(Joy looks away.)

PROFESSOR BYRNES (CONT'D)
I know it's hard. But it's best that we answer your questions now, rather than later on in life when they can really hurt you.

(Joy turns and looks at the painting.)

JOY
He is the messenger.

PROFESSOR BYRNES
What?

JOY
Like the story-teller in the last picture, He was sent by God to give us hope.

(Professor Byrnes looks back at Ahdi's painting.)

JOY (CONT'D)
… even those four children, the three girls and the little boy.

(Professor Byrnes reaches out with his bandaged hand and touches the coarse textured painting. His fingers trace the wound in Christ's side.)

PROFESSOR BYRNES
And what about the little boy? Does the girl have a message from God for him too?

JOY
I don't know.

(Professor Byrnes pulls his hand away from the painting of Christ.)

PROFESSOR BYRNES
And how are you aware of all this? Do you know this artist also?

JOY
What does it matter? It's only a painting.

(Joy turns and walks away, leaving Professor Byrnes alone. A look of sadness crosses his face as he watches Joy depart; but it is quickly replaced by one of anger as he turns his attention back toward the crucifixion scene.)

PROFESSOR BYRNES
Hmmpff. Well, *do* you have a message for me?

(The professor waits for an answer.)

PROFESSOR BYRNES (CONT'D)
I didn't think so. You were the hope of the world, and yet you ended up the poster boy for human suffering. If this is a picture of your death, then why is it called *life*?

(The tall stranger walks over to the professor.)

STRANGER
Because it doesn't end here.

PROFESSOR BYRNES
Excuse me?

STRANGER
He has risen, as he said he would.

PROFESSOR BYRNES
(sarcastically)
And I take it *you* know the artist?

STRANGER
Of *life*? Yes. I work for Him.

(The stranger walks off, leaving the professor staring at the painting.)

EXT: SCHOOL OBSERVATORY-EVENING
(Professor Byrnes meets again with Joy to address her questions of God and suffering. The two meet on the roof of a building on campus where Professor Hank is waiting to take them up to the observatory.)

PROFESSOR HANK
Hey, Jim.

PROFESSOR BYRNES
Hey, what's up Hank?

(The two men shake hands)

PROFESSOR BYNES (CONT"D)
This is Joy, the student I was telling you about. Joy, this is Professor Hank. He's in the science department here on campus and he's arranged for us to use the observatory.

PROFESSOR HANK
Joy, consider yourself lucky. Jim Byrnes hasn't shown his kind side to anyone for years. I should know; I'm his best friend.

PROFESSOR BYRNES
You like to think you are.

PROFESSOR HANK
Now, now, Jim, we used to be very close a few years back before—
well, anyway, I have to go; everything's been arranged.

PROFESSOR BYRNES
You're not joining us?

PROFESSOR HANK
No, I have a meeting with the department chair. I want to petition
him to change the school's policy on macroevolution on the
grounds that it is not truly experimental but suggestive in nature.
But you two go ahead; like I said, everything's been prepared.

PROFESSOR BYRNES
Wish I could tell you good luck, Hank, but chances are you won't
get five minutes into your petition before you're asked to leave.

JOY
(Shocked)
Professor!

PROFESSOR HANK
It's Okay, Joy. We have a mutual understanding. I remind him of
something he hates, and I hate the fact that he doesn't want to
remember.

JOY
Well, I for one can feel your sincerity.

*(Joy walks over to Professor Hank and stands directly in front of
him, her back to Prof. Byrnes.)*

JOY (CONT'D)
When you meet with that chairman, Professor, let him see your
heart as well as your cause.

(Now whispering to Prof. Hank)
—and I'm praying for you.

PROFESSOR HANK
Thank you, Joy. You were right Jim. She is something special.

(Professor Hank turns and walks off. Joy and the Professor Byrnes walk into the observatory.)

PROFESSOR BYRNES
The universe is a vast place, but we can only trust in what we see and know.

(The technician opens the panels to reveal the night sky full of stars.)

JOY
Wow!

PROFESSOR BYRNES
So, Joy, behind which star is God hiding?

JOY
Silly, God doesn't have to hide. But if I had to choose, I would say that one there.

PROFESSOR BYRNES
Why that one?

JOY
Because, it's the brightest in the sky.

PROFESSOR BYRNES
So, if God is out there, why can't we see Him?

JOY
You don't have to see Him; just like that star, we see its light and we know its there.

PROFESSOR BYRNES
Ironically, Joy, there may be *nothing* behind that light.

JOY
Is that so?

PROFESSOR BYRNES
That star may very well be dead, and the light you see, possibly millions of years old. Stars die all the time, but we don't think of it in terms of suffering. Why do you think that is Joy?

JOY
Because stars were not created in the image of God.

PROFESSOR BYRNES
Well, if there's no God, then life and death are just universal laws, and suffering is not something that must be justified, it's something that just is, whether it occurs with stars, plants or even a little child.

JOY
That doesn't seem fair, Professor.

PROFESSOR BYRNES
That's just it, the *world* is not fair, there's suffering, nor is *life* fair, there's death. These are things we just have to accept and not try to rationalize with religion.

JOY
I understand. You know, people are a lot like stars.

PROFESSOR BYRNES
Is that so?

JOY
Yes. Because when they die we can still see their light. When I was born, they told my mom and dad that I was very sick and may not live pass my fifteenth birthday. As I grew older, I used to wonder what would happen when I'm gone.

(Joy turns to the professor.)

JOY
Would my parents forget me?

PROFESSOR BYRNES
Hmmf. Never in a million years.

(Joy smiles)

JOY
How can you be so sure?

PROFESSOR BYRNES
Because, I have a daughter.

JOY
How come you never talk about her?

PROFESSOR BYRNES
She's not with me anymore.

(Joy boards the bus and heads for home. After taking her seat, she retrieves the text book the professor gave her and stares at the title. "The Illusion of God")

INT. SCHOOL CAFÉ – FOLLOWING WEEK

(Joy meets with the professor at their usual spot in the college café and notices the bandage still on his hand.)

JOY
How's your hand?

PROFESSOR BYRNES
(looking at his bandaged hand)
Something's take time to heal.

JOY
Well, I have something for you. Maybe it will help.

(Joy pulls a tie from her bag and sets it down on the table, on top of the professor's philosophy book.)

PROFESSOR BYRNES
Thank you, Joy, but I can't. It is inappropriate for teachers to accept gifts from their students. There are boundaries, you know.

JOY
What about from a friend?

PROFESSOR BYRNES
Excuse me?

JOY
Can you accept a gift from a friend? Last week you acted as a friend by helping me. I just wanted to return the favor. Besides, Paul was right. You could use a little color in your life.

(Joy pushes the book and the tie over to the professor.)

PROFESSOR BYRNES
(Smiling)
You mean a little *Joy* in my life.

JOY
Professor, you smiled again. You've been doing that a lot lately.

PROFESSOR BYRNES
Yes. But do me a favor. Don't tell anyone. I have a reputation to uphold.

(The café waitress brings over a cup of tea and sets it down before the Professor.)

WAITRESS
Would you like something darling?

JOY
No thank you.

WAITRESS
That's a nice church tie.

PROFESSOR BYRNES
I doubt if I'll be wearing it to church.

JOY
I didn't give it to you for that Professor.

WAITRESS
Darling, where's your faith?

(A saddened look crosses Joy's face and she looks away.)

PROFESSOR BYRNES
Ah—thank you. That will be all for now.

(The waitress walks off.)

JOY
She's right you know. I don't have any faith.

PROFESSOR BYRNES
Don't mind her. Belief is overrated.

(Professor Byrnes slides his cup of tea to Joy.)

PROFESSOR BYRNES (CONT'D)
Here drink up. It will make you feel better.

JOY
(smiling)
You do love tea.

PROFESSOR BYRNES
It's my daughter. Every time I came home frustrated, she would get her tea set, pour me a make believe cup, and have me read to her. It was the last thing we ever did together.

(Professor Byrnes stares at the cup of tea on the table in front of Joy.)

PROFESSOR BYRNES
When she left, I kept one tradition... but enough of that, let's get started.

INT: STUDENT UNION BUILDING-AFTERNOON

(Samantha and Holly have brought Joy to the Student Union Building where the campus clubs meet, hoping to find a Christian club that can address their troubled friend's needs. Samantha begins flipping through the many flyers on the bulletin board.)

SAMANTHA
There's got to be one here somewhere.

HOLLY
What clubs do you see?

SAMANTHA
"Islam," "Global Warming," "Lesbians," "Save the Trees—"

HOLLY
"Save the trees?" You got to be kidding me. Look at all that paper on the board.

JOY
Guys, you don't have to do this; the professor's helping me.

SAMANTHA
That's why we're doing this.

(Behind the girls, the building is filled with conversation and activity. A despondent Joy glances over into one of the meeting rooms and sees Frankie's group.)

HOLLY (CONT'D)
(Pulling Joy near her)
Oh no, you don't.

SAMANTHA
Got it! "Christian Campus Bible Fellowship." "Come study the Bible and pray. All denominations welcome."

HOLLY
All right, what room do they meet?

JOY
I'm not going.

HOLLY
Why not?

JOY
I already know what a Christian believes. I don't know how to defend it in class.

SAMANTHA
That's because—

JOY
That's because it's not real.

SAMANTHA
No, because someone's lied to you.

JOY
Yes, my mother, my father, the church. Right now I need answers.

(Joy looks over at Frankie's group)

SAMANTHA
So that's how it's going to be, huh? Well, we're not coming with you this time.

(Holly moves toward Joy, but Samantha stops her.)

JOY

Is that Christian club going to tell me why the stories in the Bible are similar to those in other cultures? Or how to respond when a teacher says the Bible contradicts science and evolution?

SAMANTHA
(Grabbing Joy's arm)
I can't answer that, Joy. But you listen to me. I don't know why God is taking you down this road, but I do know that believers don't look to the world for answers. And I know you; in your heart, Joy, you believe.

JOY
(Pulling away from Samantha)
Well, I don't, not anymore.

(Joy leaves and walks toward the room where Frankie is meeting. She pauses at the door and looks back at her two friends, then enters the room.)

SCENE MONTAGE

(Over the next few weeks, Joy continues to meet with Professor Byrnes and Frankie's group. She studies with the professor and even takes him to a men's store to buy a jacket to match his new tie. As she meets with Frankie and his group, she gives special attention to Debbie and her baby. Joy stops taking calls from her friends Samantha and Holly and her attendance in church drops until just her Bible lies on the pew between her mother and father.)

EXT. COLLEGE CAMPUS – AFTERNOON

(It is the day of Debbie's abortion and the four teens have agreed to meet on campus to accompany her. Kevin is the first to arrive. As Joy approaches, she hears two students laughing at Kevin as they walk pass him.)

STUDENT 1
(Laughing)
Take a look at him.

(The students snicker and move on.)

JOY
You ok?

KEVIN
You mean those idiots? I may not look it, but I'm a lot tougher than that.

(Joy sits down next to Kevin.)

JOY
But you're also human.

KEVIN
I bet you think somehow their ignorance is my fault.

JOY
The truth? Yes I do.

KEVIN
And why is that?

JOY
Well–

KEVIN
Let me guess, you're going to say, "God hates homosexuality but loves the homosexual," right?

JOY
(Pointing to Kevin's rainbow scarf and sneakers.)
No. I was going to say, "Maybe you need to tone it down."

(The two friends laugh.)

KEVIN
It *is* hard sometimes you know, especially with my family.

JOY
They haven't accepted you?

KEVIN
My father tries, but you can see the truth in his eyes when he looks at me and my mother, she cries all the time. I don't even know if she loves me.

JOY
Are they Christians?

KEVIN
My parents? Last time I checked they were Zen Buddhists.

(Joy and Kevin laugh.)

KEVIN (CONT'D)
I left home and didn't look back. I haven't seen them in about three years.

(Kevin drops his head)

KEVIN (CONT'D)
But don't worry; I'm going to make something of myself, despite what she thinks. But I can't help the way I was born.

JOY
I don't believe you were born that way.

KEVIN
How can you say that? They say it's genetic.

JOY
It's no more genetic than our friendship.

KEVIN
Joy, you're not the type of person I'm usually friends with. I *chose* you as a friend.

JOY
And what about those guys earlier? They don't agree with your life style either. Why aren't you friends with them?

KEVIN
The two idiots? There's nothing to build a friendship on. I've only had one experience with them and it was bad.

JOY
And I think it's the same with you. Who you are is a matter of experiences and choices.

KEVIN
Well there are some experiences that can cause a fifteen year old boy to make some *bad* choices.

(Kevin removes his lace glove to reveal the scars on his wrist.)

KEVIN
Know what's funny? Sometimes I wish I had never been born.

(Joy puts her arm around Kevin.)

JOY
Well perhaps you need to be born again.

(Frankie and Richard arrive with Debbie.)

FRANKIE
Are you two ready to go?

INT: ABORTION CLINIC – AFTERNOON

(In front of the clinic, anti-abortionist and pro choice advocates have lined up to protest. Police are also lined up to make sure the protest remains peaceful. Frankie pushes his way through the angry crowd that has gathered as Joy holds a frightened Debbie close.)

JOY
(Sarcastically)
Did you have to pick this day to schedule the abortion?

FRANKIE
Yes. This is the best day. Now you can see how crazy you Christian fanatics really are.

JOY
They're not the ones acting crazy, Frankie. The crowd is.

FRANKIE
Give them time; you'll see.

(A pro-life protestor approaches Debbie and the group.)

PRO-LIFE ADVOCATE
Do you know what you are about to do child? There are other options available to you other than ending an innocent life. God—

FRANKIE
Your God takes life! What about that?

PRO-LIFE ADVOCATE
You can't compare the actions of a desperate woman to that of a creator God.

FRANKIE
Why not? Both give life!

PRO-LIFE ADVOCATE
You are mistaken. We women give *birth*. God gives *life*.

FRANKIE
Same thing, one is getting rid of an unwanted pregnancy, the other getting rid of an unwanted life.

PRO-LIFE ADVOCATE
Well, what mother or doctor do you know after leaving a dead fetus on the operating table has the power to raise it up again?

FRANKIE
Let's get out of here.

(The group breaks through the crowd only to find a sea of teens and adults lying on the sidewalk in fetal potions. Their bodies outlined in chalk.)

DEBBIE
Oh my God. Who are they?

(Another pro-life protestor approaches Debbie and Joy.)

PRO-LIFE PROTESTOR
They are the children of women who had abortions.

DEBBIE
Who *had* abortions? How is that possible? They're alive?

PRO-LIFE PROTESTOR
Yes, they survived the procedure.

DEBBIE
I don't think I can do this.

JOY
You don't have to, Deb.

FRANKIE
Don't let these nuts intimidate you. We're right here. C'mon.

(Frankie grabs Debbie's hand and takes her inside the clinic.)

(Joy gets cut off from her group as the protestors push signs and flyers in her face.)

PRO-LIFE PROTESTOR
Did you know some of these facilities give underage children abortions and won't report cases of statutory rape?

PRO-CHOICE PROTESTOR
So what? It's the woman's right to choose.

PRO-LIFE PROTESTOR
Yes, but if she's underage, she's not a woman; she's a child.

(The pro-life protestor hands Joy some pamphlets.)

PRO-LIFE PROTESTOR
Think about it, child, please.

(Joy stares at the different pamphlets. The first one says "Norma's Story" Joy puts the pamphlets in her pocket and makes her way to the door of the clinic. Inside, the others are registering Debbie at the desk.)

JOY
Frankie, you can't force her to do this. It's un—

FRANKIE
What? Ungodly? I thought you were through with that nonsense. Besides, we're just here for support.

JOY
This is not support, this is pressure.

FRANKIE
Wait now, I didn't pressure her, this was her idea.

(Debbie looks away.)

JOY
Where's the father? She didn't make this baby by herself.

FRANKIE
What difference does it make where the father is? Roe vs. Wade.
It's the *woman's* choice.

JOY
(remembering the pamphlet)
Her real name was Norma McCorvey and she made her choice.
She never had the abortion. She's a Christian mother of three. She
chose life and she chose God and Debbie should be free to make
her choice too. And when she chooses God, abortion will be a decision she will always regret.

RICHARD
Joy, abortion is a safe and legal way to end a pregnancy; it says so
in this brochure. That's why it's called Planned Parenthood.

JOY
It might as well be called planned murder, because you are killing
millions of innocent children.

FRANKIE
Joy, two things. One, if God exists, He definitely wouldn't approve
of abortion, so for me, God does not exist. That way, I don't worry
about Him judging my actions. And two, that *thing* in her stomach
is not human yet, so I don't look at it as killing.

DEBBIE
I'm feeling pain.

KEVIN
Deb, you need to calm down.

(Debbie puts a cigarette to her mouth.)

DEBBIE
I'm going for a smoke.

(Joy grabs some pro-choice flyers from off the rack. As she walks towards Debbie, she switches them with the pro-life pamphlets in her pocket that she received from the protestor outside.)

JOY
(Snatching the cigarette from Debbie's mouth)
Here, read a pamphlet.

(The two girls stare at each other.)

(Debbie then looks at the pamphlet. The panels are filled with mutilated bodies of infants, surgically removed by abortion. The heading reads "In a moment, the nurse will come in and ask you "Are you ready." Turn to the baby inside of you, and ask it the same thing.)

DEBBIE
(Whispering to herself)
She's not an *it*. My baby is a girl.

NURSE
Everything's prepared. Ms. Mitchell, are you ready?

(Debbie begins to cry.)

FRANKIE
You'll be okay. We're here for you.

DEBBIE
(Looking at Joy)
Joy?

JOY
I'm coming in there, with you.

NURSE
You can't. She has to be alone with the doctor. I'm sorry.

JOY
I'll only be a moment, I swear.

NURSE
Okay. You can help her get undressed.

(Joy grabs Debbie.)

JOY
Look at me, girl. It's going to be okay. You hear me? I promise.

DEBBIE
(Wiping her tears)
Yes.

JOY
Follow me.

(As the two girls leave, Frankie and the others look outside at the protestors.)

RICHARD
Man, it's crazy out there.

KEVIN
Yeah! You'd think someone was dying in here.

(Richard slaps Kevin in the back of his head.)

RICHARD
Jack ass!

FRANKIE
Everyone has the right to choose Kevin, including Deb. If she wants to get rid of that child, it's her right, and these protestors are trying to stop her from doing that. The police need to break them up.

(Frankie moves towards the door.)

RICHARD
Hey man, where you going?

FRANKIE
To join the resistance.

(Moments later, Joy returns to the waiting room.)

JOY
Where's Frankie?

KEVIN
You mean Che Guevara? He's outside, yelling at Christians.

(Suddenly, the crowd outside begins to run.)

JOY
What's going on?

RICHARD
I don't know? But the police are everywhere.

(The nurse comes in from the other room.)

NURSE
Everyone must leave the building now, there is a bomb threat.

KEVIN
What about Deb?

NURSE
The patients are being brought back out; I'll go and see about your friend.

(Frankie comes back in the building.)

FRANKIE
See. I told you Joy. Your Christians are nothing but a bunch of crazed fanatics.

(The nurse comes back in the room.)

NURSE
Your friend is not back there in the prep room.

RICHARD
So where the hell is she?

NURSE
I don't know. There was one girl on the table when the bomb was called in. The doctors are removing her fetus now.

KEVIN
We're waiting.

NURSE
No, everyone must evacuate now.

(The guards and staff usher the four teens out the building.)

INT: HISTORY DEPT. TEACHERS LOUNGE-AFTERNOON

(Joy goes into the history department to meet with Prof. Byrnes. She steps off the elevator onto the fourth floor and hears the professor's voice coming from down the hall. She walks toward the teacher's lounge to find him arguing with Prof. Hank.)

PROFESSOR HANK
There is a curriculum for the course Jim; you can't just stand in front of a classroom full of students and openly deny God.

PROFESSOR BYRNES
And why not? They have been pampered all their life by their parents, and it's our job to prepare them for the real world.

PROFESSOR HANK
The real world?

PROFESSOR BYRNES
Yes. And in the real world, there's no place for fairy tales of floods, and there's definitely no room for God!

PROFESSOR HANK
Just because you're an atheist doesn't mean they have to be also! They are not just students occupying a chair, they're people and many of them believe in a God. A God that's real, a God that loves them, and takes care of them. And you have no right to take that away from them!

PROFESSOR BYRNES
Oh yeah! Well where was your loving God when I needed him? Where was he for my little girl?

(*Joy sticks her head into the room.*)

JOY
Is everything all right, Professor?

(*The two men turn to Joy.*)

PROFESSOR BYRNES
(*Looking at Hank*)
Your belief in God sickens me.

(*Professor Byrnes gets up and grabs his things, but Prof. Hank reaches out and grabs his arm.*)

PROFESSOR HANK
Jim, wait.

PROFESSOR BYRNES
(Pulling away from Hank)
You follow your heart, I'll follow my mind.

(Professor Byrnes walks out the room.)

JOY
(Looking at Prof. Hank)
You haven't given him a reason to believe; but something obviously has given him a reason not to.

PROFESSOR HANK
You're on his side?

JOY
I understand him.

PROFESSOR HANK
And now *I* understand. Go.

(Joy runs down the hall after Professor Byrnes.)

JOY
Professor, wait!

PROFESSOR BYRNES
This isn't a good time, Joy.

(Joy follows the professor into his office and closes the door.)

JOY
This is about your daughter, right? She didn't go away, did she? She died?

PROFESSOR BYRNES
I don't want to talk about it Joy. Leave it alone.

(Professor Byrnes begins to pace the room.)

PROFESSOR BYRNES (CONT'D)
God is great, God is good— If He's so good, then why didn't he answer?!

JOY
I-I don't know.

PROFESSOR BYRNES
I'll tell you why; because he does not exist. Because belief is a waste of time and because she was sick and people who are sick die all the time.

(Professor Byrnes angrily shoves all the papers from his desk.)

PROFESSOR BYRNES (CONT'D)
In the real world, those who mean the world to you die and leave you all alone.

(Professor Byrnes collapses to the floor.)

JOY
Professor, are you ok?

PROFESSOR BYRNES
(Looking up at Joy)
I never even had the chance to say good-bye to her.

EXT:CEMETERY: AFTERNOON-IMMEDIATELY AFTER

(Joy has gone with Professor Byrnes to his daughter's gravesite, to help him say goodbye.)

PROFESSOR BYNES
I don't know about this, Joy.

JOY
Go ahead, Professor. It's best that you face it now rather than later.

Isn't that what you told me?

PROFESSOR BYRNES
Yes, it is.

CUT TO:
HEADSTONE

(The name on the headstone reads "Faith Nicole Byrnes 1998–2003")

PROFESSOR BYRNES
I can't do this, Joy.

JOY
It's Okay Professor. Take my hand.

(Joy takes hold of the professor's bandaged hand.)

PROFESSOR BYRNES
I . . . I've . . . missed you.

(Professor Byrnes's eyes begin to fill with tears.)

PROFESSOR BYRNES (CONT'D)
I've tried to move on, to forget, but I can't; you're everywhere. I see you in other little children, in my dreams. Even at home I still hear your voice—

(The professor lets go of Joy's hand.)

PROFESSOR BYRNES
This is silly, I shouldn't be doing this.

JOY
(Taking hold of his hand)
It's Okay, Professor, go on.

PROFESSOR BYRNES
(Wiping his eyes)
You know, I still remember that day as if it were yesterday. I remember sitting in your room; we were reading the . . . hmff.

(Professor Byrnes looks to Joy and squeezes her hand.)

PROFESSOR BYRNES (CONT'D)
I remember the last words you said to me. Daddy, help me. And I remember . . . there was nothing I could do.

(Tears run uncontrollably down the professor's face.)

PROFESSOR BYRNES CONT'D
But I'll always love you. And you'll always be my little girl, my little Faith; and I'm sorry. Daddy's sorry, for trying to forget you.

(Joy moves in close and puts her arm around the professor. Above them, storm clouds begin to rise.)

INT. JOY'S HOUSE. - LATER THAT DAY.

(A storm is raging outside as Joy's father sits in the living room looking at pictures of his daughter in a photo album. Mr. Hunter lifts his head up from the album and looks around the empty room. He imagines little Joy running to him, jumping up in his lap, and asking him to read the Bible to her. Suddenly, the front door opens and Mr. Hunter and the little girl seated on his lap look up at a seventeen-year-old Joy entering the house. As she walks by her father, the image of the little girl fades from his lap.)

MR. HUNTER
Joy, where are you going? You don't just walk into a house without telling us you're home?

JOY
I'm home.

MR. HUNTER
Huh! Anyway, you have company.

JOY
Is it the pastor? I told you I don't want to see him!

(Joy's mother comes in from the kitchen.)

JOY (CONT'D)
Why can't any of you respect my wishes?

MR. HUNTER
What's gotten into you? Nowadays no one can say two words to you without you blowing up. Is that what that professor is teaching you in college; to be disrespectful to your parents? What kind of a sick old man meets with young girls after school, anyway, and tries to fill their head with foolishness and poison their hearts against their parents?

JOY
It's not like that, Daddy, and you're the one who's sick if you think that of me.

MR. HUNTER
It's what I think about him! You're just being used. He sees you as a silly young girl that he can manipulate.

MRS. HUNTER
Your father didn't mean what he said. Did you, Dwayne?

MR. HUNTER
Like hell I didn't! The Bible says honor your father and mother that your days may be long upon the earth. The pastor says it's the first commandment with promise.

JOY
The Bible was written by man.

MR. HUNTER
Yes, and that man was Moses, a prophet of God.

JOY
No, Daddy, the professor taught us that there was no such person as Moses, and that the priestly class just copied those things from earlier sources in order to control the people.

MR. HUNTER
What? Moses did not exist? Earlier sources? What earlier sources?

JOY
The code of Hammurabi.

MR. HUNTER
The code of what? Hamma who?

(Joy's father picks up a Bible from off the table.)

MR. HUNTER (CONT'D)
Joy, the Bible is the inspired word of God.

JOY
Which God, Daddy? Horus, El, Mithra?

MR. HUNTER
Jehovah God! Jesus God!

JOY
Oh, you mean Yahweh. The professor tells us that the only reason the Hebrew deity is so dominant is because it was accepted by the Europeans through Christianity and forced upon the rest of us as the Europeans conquered the world.

MR. HUNTER
You think you're pretty smart? Huh? You've never talked like this before. You think you're better than me because you took some stupid course in college? You think *he's* better than me.

JOY
No, Daddy, it's not like that. You should meet him. He can teach you a lot. The professor says—

MR. HUNTER
Enough!

(Joy jumps.)

MR. HUNTER (CONT'D)
Enough with the professor. The professor this. The professor that. It's like he's some kind of god. It's like you've replaced Jesus with this man.

(Joy looks at her father sternly and drops her head.)

MR. HUNTER (CONT'D)
Oh, that's it huh. He's your new savior. You hear this, Mel? You hear your daughter?

MRS. HUNTER
Yes. I . . . I think we should pray.

JOY
I don't want to pray.

(Mrs. Hunter looks at her daughter.)

JOY (CONT'D)
For what?

MR. HUNTER
Mel, you hear this? Our daughter doesn't want to pray with us. Because that devil of a professor is stealing her from me!

JOY
Leave him out of this, Daddy.

MR. HUNTER
You take his side over your parents, your own flesh and blood? What do you think, Mel? Do you think that professor knows he's turning our daughter against us? Do you think he even cares? He's messing with your mind, Joy. Taking you from your family! Your friends! And the God of your youth. He's a devil!

JOY
He's not a devil, Daddy! The professor has done nothing but help me. And it's you, Daddy, who has played with my mind. You and Mommy raised me to believe in a God that does not exist and let me put my faith in—in—trinkets, like this cross that can't help me.

(Joy rips the chain from her neck.)

MRS. HUNTER
Joy, no . . .

JOY
Yes, mom. I put all my hope in this and it never came through for me. I'm still sick. I still suffer. I'm still in pain.

(Joy reaches into her pocket.)

JOY (CONT'D)
And I still have to take these damn pills!

MR. HUNTER
(Slamming the Bible on the floor)
Joy, you watch your mouth!

JOY
You can't control me with that any more, Daddy! What the professor said to me makes sense, and he was right. I don't have to listen to you or believe in that anymore.

MR. HUNTER
We didn't send you to college to become an atheist! That's not what we taught you!

JOY
That's right! That's not what you taught me! You taught me to
believe in superstitions and myths! You taught me to believe in stories that I couldn't even justify in front of my class! And you taught
me to love something that's not even real!

MR. HUNTER
Enough! This is my house and you will respect God.

JOY
Dad, you don't understand. How can I respect something that I'm
not even sure exists!

MR. HUNTER
You better watch your mouth—

JOY
Or what, you'll slap me again, because you love me so much?

(Joy's mother attempts to go to her.)

JOY (CONT'D)
Stop mom, please. I've made my decision. I don't need this anymore.

*(Joy motions to throw away the cross, and Holly and Samantha
come in from the kitchen. Surprised to see them and not Pastor
Rogers, Joy turns and runs out the house, and into the storm. The
narrator begins to speak.)*

PROFESSOR BYRNES (NARRATOR)
When I was a boy, I recklessly threw pebbles into the water and
watched the ripples spread outward to the sea. Though I did it a
hundred times, I always knew what the effect would be. As educators, our words too can cause ripples in the lives of our students,
but we are not aware of these effects.

(Joy runs to her church and lies at the foot of the cross that is in the courtyard. As the rain falls on her face, she cries out to God, but the sounds of thunder and lightning drown out her screams.)

PROFESSOR BYRNES (NARRATOR)
As an educator, I never knew I had so great a responsibility.

****
End of Act III

Chapter Four

Red light.

Paul's foot sat firmly on the brake of his silver SUV as he waited at the intersection for the light to change. The muffled sounds of a song could be heard thumping from the car in back of him.

C'mon Paul; get your head right. He thought. *You're two blocks away from the church.*

Paul looked up the street at the large edifice; it's height seemed to stretch into the heavens. *Wow! I wonder if the pastors of these mega churches know how nervous they make people like me feel?*

"You can do this," he reassured himself. "You've been up all night going over your presentation. Besides they're only men and God has not given us a spirit of fear."

Green light.

"God has not given us a spirit of fear…God has not given us a spirit of fear…"

Beeeeep!

"Hey! Act like you got somewhere to go!" yelled a voice from behind.

A black mustang came from behind and pulled up slowly along side Paul's SUV. The tinted windows lowered and the music came screaming out the speakers at Paul.

"You better lose yourself in the music, the moment, you own it, you better never let it go. You only get one shot, do not miss your chance to blow, cause opportunity comes once in a life time yo…"

Vrrrooommm! And just like that, the mustang was gone.

Paul took his foot off the brake and pressed on the gas. Within minutes he pulled into the parking lot of the mega church. Other than the fact that he was nervous and extremely tired, everything was going according to plan. He had ten minutes to find parking before service started and afterwards, he would make his presentation before one of the greatest Pastors on the east coast.

Paul parked his car and headed toward the main entrance. His own church was considerably smaller, a hundred members at best; but walking into this building , was like walking into a Christian city. There were coffee shops, book stores, lounge areas, and believers of all ages bustling about. After a few inquiries, Paul found the sanctuary and walked over to one of the ushers.

"Hello, my name is Paul Agard. I have an appointment to see your Pastor after service."

"Yes, Mr. Agard, I'll inform Pastor that you've arrived," the usher responded.

"Please sit here and I'll come back to get you when he's ready to see you."

Paul took his seat and looked around the massive sanctuary.

"Lose yourself in the music, the moment, you own it, you better never let it go— "

The song from the black mustang lingered in Paul's mind as he tried to estimate how many people were in attendance.

"Two—four—eight...There must be over ten thousand people in here."

There was something comforting about having so many people who believed in God in one place. It was a feeling that anything was possible. Paul sat back in the chair and his eyes grew heavy as the choir took the stage. The morning hymn filled the sanctuary, but still the song from the black mustang played over and over in his head.

"Do not miss your chance to blow cause opportunity comes once in a life time—"

"Excuse me, Mr. Agard,"

"Oh—yes?"

"The Pastor will see you now."

Paul had drifted off for a moment.

"Please come this way."

Paul gathered his things quickly and followed the usher.

"I thought he was going to see me after service?"

"After this service, he and his colleagues have a conference to attend. But he does have fifteen minutes in which he can see you *now*."

Fifteen minutes. That's not enough time. Paul thought to himself. *Usually there's five minutes of small talk, leaving ten minutes for the presentation. Now I know why I took that film class.*

The usher lead Paul to a separate wing of the church. Down the hall, a set of large double doors were all that stood between Paul and his destiny.

Fifteen minutes; open strong; remember, you only get one shot.

The doors to the Pastors meeting room opened to reveal a sea of distinguished clergy and Christian personalities sitting at the long table. This was more than Paul expected when his contact said he would arrange the meeting. The host Pastor rose from his seat to welcome Paul.

"Gentlemen, please, don't stand," Paul quickly stated while looking at the tops of their heads, too nervous to look at their faces.

"To men like yourself, time is a precious thing, and it is not my intention to be labeled a time thief."

The usher walked out, and the double doors closed loudly behind Paul; but the sound did not break his stride.

"Let me assure you, in the short time that we have, I will do my very best to be like 1010 WINS. You give me 15 minutes—"

"Like the slogan for the radio station, *You'll give us the world?*" said a voice from the table.

Paul stopped and looked at the man to his left.

"No. I am not able to do that. But I am able to give you the next great revival in the Christian world."

Now, Thought Paul. *Lose yourself.*

In twelve minutes and fifteen seconds Paul was done. Now, he looked at the faces of the men seated at the table. They were men that he had grown up with spiritually. Christian radio personalities, theologians, pastors, and Christian family psychologists. These men were his heroes. This was more than he had ever expected.

"And who will be your target audience?"

"Where do you plan to show this film?"

"What about a distributor?"

The questions came hard and fast from the table.

"Now, now, gentleman," said the host pastor. "Let's give Mr. Agard a chance to answer."

Though Paul was nervous, he was prepared. He had done this all before in Ms. Lions class; and the fact that they were asking questions meant they may be interested.

So much for the fifteen minutes, he thought to himself. *Any thing I left out of my presentation I'll address with my answers.*

"There are three hundred million people in America." Paul proclaimed. "Of which ninety percent believe in God. If done right, that's a target audience of two hundred and seventy million."

"How so?" said the Christian Radio Host.

Paul folded his nervous hands behind his back and moved farther into the room, now walking along the right side of the table.

"Every year, millions of Americans enter into secular colleges. Jehovah witnesses, Muslims, as well as Jews. All having their faith challenged in these arenas of higher learning. *Our movie,* gentleman, makes its appeal to the believer; of which there are two hundred and seventy million in this country; each, having the right to believe."

"We can market it as, *"The film every believer must see before sending their children to college,"* said the Christian Psychologist.

The Psychologist's words filled Paul with a small burst of hope.

That's one, he thought. *Cater to him and hopefully I can win the rest of the room.*

"Yes, but what good is having a target audience if you can't get the movie into theatres?" asked one of the Pastors. "*Your film,* Mr. Agard, may have too great a religious overtone for Hollywood. If it does, where would you plan on showing it?"

"In *your* church," Paul answered.

"In my church?"

Paul's hands quickly came from behind his back.

"Yes, and in fourteen hundred and ninety-nine other churches across America."

"And you know fifteen hundred pastors that would let you do this?" Another pastor challenged.

"No, I don't; but you gentlemen do."

"Let's get down to the main question," said the Theologian. "Budget. How much would this project cost?"

"Nothing sir."

"Come again."

"Nothing. Not a cent. I am not here asking you gentlemen for money, I'm here asking you gentlemen to be the catalyst of the next great revival in America; a revival of Biblical truths and the preservation of believers' rights."

"And how do you plan to make a major motion picture for nothing?" The Theologian asked doubtfully.

"There are three things needed to make a film. Talent, equipment, and services; and you gentlemen have all three at your disposal. You have the cameras, the software, and the technicians. How much do you charge yourself to use your own equipment?"

"Nothing," answered the Christian Psychologist.

"Exactly, and as for the talent and other services, you gentlemen have an endless pool of resources, through the audiences that you command," Paul contended. "A great community of believers that look to you for guidance; and within this community are actors, directors, and producers, who would be proud to work on a project like this, with men such as you."

Paul now walked along the left side of the table.

"We will ask the Christian community across America to donate their talents, services, and resources toward making this film. We will document the whole thing—"

"A Christian reality show," interjected one of the Pastors.

"Yes." Paul continued. "The auditions, the making of the film, their stories; giving them nationwide exposure, in exchange for their services. Tickets can be sold in advance, just like a seminar. And a zero budget equals maximum profit. Also, upon completion of the film, we will hold a banquet, in which we can acknowledge and even be a blessing to all those who played a part."

"So you intend for us to shut down our churches for three months while the film is showing," said another the Pastor.

"On the contrary, I would like for you to *open* your churches to your community for two weeks. Three, seventy-five seat showings a day; on Sunday afternoon only one. After which, you can have a Q&A session where you distribute resources that will help equip your audience. I'm talking about a nationwide evangelical movement. If you're a businessman, plug in the numbers and do the math. If your an evangelist, imagine the number souls.

By now, Paul had walked around the whole table, and stood at the same place where he began his introduction.

"I see your vision young man.," said the Christian Radio Host and Apologist. "This is just the start. I could have my staff prepare a book for students entering into college that addresses all the controversial issues that they will face."

"We could also create an apologetics course, a curriculum to be offered in colleges and in Bible schools," said the Host Pastor.

"Or at least made available on campus as a resource," said the Theologian.

"Indeed. As well as in our churches and made available to families," said the Christian Psychologist.

"A pre-emptive approach that leaves our youth equip for college. I like it," said the Christian Radio Host.

The pastor at the end of the table to Paul's left, shook his head, "If this thing is done right, it could be—"

Paul interjected. "The next great revival in the Christian world."

"Yes, I guess it could."

Paul seized the moment.

"Gentleman. Make no mistake about it. I am standing before some of the most notable names in Christendom today. Some of you command thousands locally and millions nationally. Individually, any project you embrace is a success. Collectively, anything you embrace is a movement. If the favor of God has allowed you to have influence over so many people, then you can use this as an opportunity to equip them biblically and protect their right to believe. For too long self interest and corruption has plagued our country, in all areas, the church included; leaving this nation on the brink of an economic and spiritual depression. But even now, new coalitions have formed to lift our nation out of ruin; but who will be that light for the church? Gentlemen, the people are hungry for revival! Make no mistake about it, this year, change is coming; politically, economically and if you great men of God will lead us, spiritually. But an opportunity like this, may only come once in a life time—"

"Excuse me, Mr. Agard."

"Oh— yes?"
"The Pastor will see you now."
Paul had drifted off for a moment.

****

Act IV

The Return of Joy

INT: DOCTOR OFFICE-MORNING

(Joy and Mrs. Hunter sit in the doctor's office and the family physician walks in with the latest results from Joy's test.)

JOY
Well, what's my tests say?

DOCTOR FOSTER
Hello Mrs. Hunter. Hello Joy.

JOY'S MOTHER
Hello doctor.

DOCTOR FOSTER
So Joy, How are you doing?

JOY
That's why I'm here. So you can tell me.

DOCTOR FOSTER
No, not physically. I mean your life, your friends.

JOY
Why do you ask? Has my mother been talking to you about me?

DOCTOR FOSTER
No, it's just that usually you'd have about a dozen tracts hidden for me through out my office; but today, you just want to hear the results of your test.

JOY
Well, what do they say?

DOCTOR FOSTER
Some of your levels are off, which isn't very good.

(Joy drops her head and Mrs. Hunter places her arm around her.)

DOCTOR FOSTER (CONT'D)
That's why I'm curious as to if you're doing something different in your life. I hear you've started college; that's a big milestone for us. Maybe a little too big?

JOY
I'll be outside.

(Joy gets up and walks out the doctor's office.)

JOY'S MOTHER
Some things are different.

DOCTOR FOSTER
I suspected so.

INT. CLASSROOM - AFTERNOON ONE WEEK LATER

(Joy's unhappiness draws the attention of her fellow student.)

STUDENT 1
Hey. What's up, Joy?

JOY
Hey.

STUDENT 1
What's wrong?

JOY
Nothing.

STUDENT 1
You sure? You look pretty upset.

JOY
You wouldn't understand.

STUDENT 1
Try me.

JOY
I don't know; this whole religion thing. Have you ever felt like…
someone was forcing you to do something you didn't want to do?

STUDENT 1
And now you feel violated.

JOY
Yes.

(Frankie joins the conversation.)

FRANKIE
So who stole it from you?

JOY
Who stole my what?

FRANKIE
Your "*joy*"—Joy. Who stole your *joy*?

JOY
Very funny.

STUDENT 1
Well, who was it? I mean, I know the professor might seem incon-
siderate at times, but—

JOY
It's not the professor. Never mind.

(The professor begins to speak.)

PROFESSOR BYRNES
In 63 B.C.E., the title Pontifex Maximus, makes its way into the
Roman Imperial office with Julius Caesar among others. Here we

see another union of church and state and all the consequences that come with it. But ironically his constituents felt him too powerful and Gaius led an assassination plot to kill him.

(Professor Byrnes turns and writes a name on the board.)

PROFESSOR BYRNES (CONT'D)
Cassius Longinus. Most accounts have *him* as the primary conspirator. But, Just like Jesus, it is a story of betrayal, with Brutus, Caesar's close friend leading the assassination plot against him. In any case, as the head of state and now religious priest, the Caesars instituted such practices as paying tribune and emperor worship. And in America today, we still fight to separate this cultural mixture of oil and water—church and state. Our modern society, ladies and gentlemen, is one of new ideas, free ideas and the fables and myths of religion cannot be forced upon the state and used to govern our society.

PAUL
It would seem that the three most influential people that exist are world leaders and religious leaders.

PROFESSOR BYRNES
For once, Mr. Agard, you are right.

(The class laughs and Joy also smiles.)

PROFESSOR BYRNES (CONT'D)
And who is the third?

PAUL
The educator.

CLASS
Ooooh.

(Upset with Paul's comment, Joy raises her hand. The professor looks sternly at Paul, but turns to Joy as she calls on him.)

JOY
Professor, All my life my parents raised me to be a Christian and to read the Bible. But after taking your class, I no longer believe in it. And now I argue with my mother and father day and night, to the point where we yell and scream at each other. Professor, please, won't you come to my house and convince my parents that Christianity is a lie?

PAUL
What!?

PROFESSOR BYRNES
My sympathy goes out to you, Joy. But people like your parents who believe in faith are so superstitious that they will never listen to science. And subsequently, scientists never believe in things like faith. The two cannot be reconciled.

PAUL
My god! Is no one else in this class offended? Are none of you going to say anything? I mean forget me. He's talking about your faith too!

PROFESSOR BYRNES
It's not my fault that you grew up on a book filled with contradictions and not one based on history. That's why you're in college; to correct that.

PAUL
What right do you have to say that to us? This is America, and the constitution gives us the right to believe.

PROFESSOR BYRNES
We've done this dance already Mr. Agard. I can give you scores of contradictions in that book. Joshua, Matthews, even Genesis. None of them can stand up to literary criticism.

PAUL
It doesn't matter what example you use to discredit the Bible; your reasoning is fundamentally flawed.

PROFESSOR BYRNES
How so?

PAUL
You can't ask an author who lived over thirty-five hundred years ago to adhere to the literary laws of the twenty-first century.

FRANKIE
Certain writing laws are universal. The creation stories in the Old Testament, they just don't add up and the *JEPD Theory* tells us why.

STUDENT 1
What's the JEPD Theory?

PROFESSOR BYRNES
A well founded theory that claims Moses did not write the Pentateuch, four separate   authors did.

PAUL
So, you're familiar with Wellhausen? Then you know *he's* come under some criticism too. His methods were suspect. To make his theory stand, he literally reconstructed Jewish history and disregarded evidence in the text that would discredit him.

FRANKIE
Bull! The book of Genesis *proves* the theory. In one story, the author uses the name *Jehovah* for God and in the other story; a second author uses the name *Elohim*. Two different names! Two different authors!

PAUL
What about Genesis 28:13? "I am *Jehovah Elohim*, the God, of Abraham, the God of Isaac." Here, the author uses both Yahweh and Elohim in the same sentence. Two different names; one author.

(Joy's eyes open wide.)

JOY
Oh, God…No!

FRANKIE
It doesn't matter. A writer should be consistent about the details
when telling a story—

JOY
Yes, otherwise it can confuse the reader. Isn't that right professor?

PROFESSOR BYRNES
An irrefutable point Joy, don't you think so Mr. Agard?

PAUL
Professor, earlier you told us, that *Gaius* lead the plot to assassinate
Julius Caesar.

PROFFESOR BYRNES
He did.

PAUL
But moments later, when you retold the story, you contradicted
yourself by stating that it was a man named *"Cassius Longinus"*
and then *"Brutus"* who led the plot to assassinate Caesar. Which
one was it, Gaius, Cassius Longinus, or Brutus?

PROFESSOR BYRNES
I did not contradict myself. It was Gaius who hatched the plot, he
was also called *"Cassius Longinus"* but on the *day* of the coup, it
was *"Brutus"* who led the actual assassination. Everyone knows
this. If you had done the reading, you would have too.

PAUL
I apologize for my ignorance. I should have known you were utilizing different names of the *one* character and that your goal was
to highlight specific points of the story and not necessarily to
explain facts already established.

(Paul turns to Joy.)

PAUL (CON'T)
Maybe Moses and the Bible writers were doing the same?

(Joy scrambles for her bible and flips through the pages.)

(Paul turns back to the professor.)

PAUL (CONT'D)
And *their* contemporaries would have understood this and been aware of the *facts* that stump us three millenniums later.

FRANKIE
And what about the different styles Wellhausen spoke of?

PAUL
Again, there is no archeological evidence that verifies any of Wellhausen's assumptions. In essence, they're his opinions. He's entitled to them, but they're unfounded claims and Bible critics, who ignorantly follow Wellhausen, interpret different styles to be the work of different authors instead of it being the work of one author utilizing different styles.

JOY
(whispering to herself)
One author...utilizing different styles.

PAUL
It's funny, you blindly accept the works of Wellhausen, a mere man; and you subject God's word to an un-passable test. We stand in awe of the world shapers, when it's the world *maker* we need to respect; for God alone who has the power to give life and to take it. An irrefutable point, don't you think so professor?

(Professor Byrnes' runs his fingers across the picture of his daughter which sticks out from within the pages of his book. His face hardens as he reads the title that lies just beneath his daughters face... "The Illusion of God" The professor pushes his daughters picture downward till it disappears into the book.)

PROFESSOR BYRNES
From history, we learn to move forward and religion is nothing more than a speed bump on the road to this country's progress. As a nation we are finally beginning to acknowledge this and remove it from our society. The belief in God has infiltrated our courts, our culture, and even our Pledge of Allegiance.

PAUL
And that's your goal, isn't it, Professor? To take us back three hundred years and strip us of our constitutional rights?

PROFESSOR BYRNES
What rights? You do not have the right to superimpose what you believe in your home on me.

(Paul stands to his feet.)

PAUL
And you, Professor, do not have the right to superimpose your unbelief on me and what I have believed in my home!

(Joy reaches into her bag for her Bible.)

JOY
How could I?

PAUL
You have no consideration for the rights of those you teach. Students, whether they believe in God or not, are invited in to classes like these, and men like you perform a secular date rape on our religious rights.

PROFESSOR BYRNES
Secular date raping of your religious rights? That's quite some analogy.

PAUL
Yes it is, because just like date rape, we came to this class trusting the integrity of the institution and you, the professor, who we just met.

PROFESSOR BYRNES
And?

(Paul moves toward the professor.)

PAUL
You used this class as a platform to inject us with your anti-Christian rhetoric.

(The professor motions to a student.)

PROFESSOR BYRNES
Go and call security.

(The student hurries out the room.)

PROFESSOR BYRNES
As I said at the beginning of the semester, this is not high school. You are adults now. The nature of the discussions are far more mature. You can call it rape if you want to, Mr. Agard, but this class is my house, and when you come in here, as naive as you might be, there is a little thing that I have, called academic freedom. Teachers are entitled to freely discuss the findings of their studies. No one has raped you. You signed up for college. You took this class. What did you expect?

PAUL
You speak of academic freedom? Then you know teachers should be careful not to introduce into their lesson controversial matter that has no relation to their subject. You've violated us. We came to learn history; instead you taught us atheism.

STUDENT 2
Son, you need to relax.

(Paul turns on the students.)

PAUL
Did any of you come into this class expecting to have your personal beliefs challenged? Did any of you come into this history class ready to argue the existence of God? Did you?

STUDENT 2
No.

PAUL
Then the problem is that *you* are too relaxed.

(The student comes back in the room with security.)

SECURITY
Is there a problem, Professor?

PROFESSOR BYRNES
Is there a problem Mr. Agard?

(Paul gathers his things and tosses his Bible at Professor Byrnes who catches it in the chest.)

PAUL
(Pointing at the class)
Yes, their faith in your hands.

(Frankie looks at Paul as he leaves and shakes his head in anger.)

FRANKIE
(Speaking to himself)
You're about to get a taste of your own medicine.

(Frankie looks out the classroom window where students are gathering for Tolerance Day.)

FRANKIE (CONT'D)
See you on the battlefield.

EXT. CAMPUS GROUNDS - IMMEDIATELY AFTER CLASS

(A large crowd of students, faculty, and onlookers have gathered for Tolerance day. From an elevated stage, each group takes turns representing their own political, cultural, or social view.)

GAY ACTIVIST
There is no longer a place for oppression in our country. We *will* be accepted!

(The crowd cheers.)

GAY ACTIVIST
And we who fill these classrooms and graduate from these colleges are the leaders of tomorrow. America, look at your future!

(As the crowd roars, the gay activists step away from the mic and Paul's group steps to the podium. They're each wearing their signature "I have the right to believe" T-shirts. The leaders of the group, Peter and Lisa, have brought their four-year-old son along. Joy, too, is in the crowd with Kevin and Richard, but she tries to hide her face from Samantha and Holly, who are also on the stage. Lisa steps to the mic and begins to speak.)

LISA
Yes we are the future. But as leaders, we have a responsibility, a responsibility to each other and to our God.

(Frankie makes his way through the crowd and stands just behind Joy; his eyes fixate on Paul and his group.)

FRANKIE
Hey, Joy.

(Joy notices Frankie is concealing something beneath his overcoat.)

JOY
Hey.

(From the stage, Samantha and Holly notice Joy in the crowd.)

LISA
And behind these walls, our religious rights are being stripped from us by secular institutions that have no respect for God.

ATHEIST IN CROWD
This is Tolerance Day, not Jesus day!

LISA
And we who believe in God have a voice too.

(Some members of the crowd begin to turn on Paul's group.)

GAY ACTIVIST
What about my rights? I'm gay!

LISA
This is not that type of meeting. We're not here for that.

(Lisa's husband, Peter, gets nervous.)

PETER
I don't like this, Paul. It's like some kind of wild west showdown.

PAUL
Yeah. Like the movie "Tombstone," Clantons vs. the Earps.

(Paul steps forward and moves Lisa back with her husband and child.)

PAUL
You heard the lady. It's not that type of meeting. But if you still want to dance, I'm your huckleberry.

GAY ACTIVIST
It's the church that won't allow two consenting adults to marry! What kind of tolerance is that?

PAUL
It's the church that won't allow two consenting *homosexuals* to marry.

GAY ACTIVIST
Listen to you. That word. "Homosexual." We're people, you know.

PAUL
Christians didn't invent that word, a gay activist, *Karl Maria Benkert* did, any more questions from the crowd?

(Some of the members in the crowd begin to yell at Paul's group. Frankie pushes Joy to the ground and rushes toward the stage. He rips open his overcoat to reveal a string of plastic canisters strapped to his torso. He makes his way up the steps and throws himself at the stage. He screams four words that center everyone's attention.)

FRANKIE
There is no god!

(The crowd runs for cover and Peter tries to guard his wife and child but is too late.)

BOOM!!!

(The smoke slowly clears. Everyone on the stage is covered in red.)

LISA
AAAAIIIIEEEEE!!

(Peter and Lisa's son lies motionless on the stage, stained with the strange red substance.)

LISA
He's dead! He's dead!

(Peter frantically wipes away the red liquid, looking for his son's wounds but finds none. The child opens his eyes and coughs.)

LISA
Peter, is he—

(They realize it was a hoax. In a fit of rage, Peter turns on Frankie.)

PETER
You monster!

(Peter rushes for Frankie and the two men fall off the stage to the ground. The campus police arrive to bring order. Joy runs from the scene and her friends follow.)

EXT. CAMPUS BATHROOM - IMMEDIATELY AFTER.

(Samantha and Holly catch up with Joy.)

JOY
I had nothing to do with that!

SAMANTHA
We know. But you were with him.

JOY
I wasn't with him, he was just there. Anyway, you can't tell me who I can hang out with.

SAMANTHA
Yeah, I know, but you used to hang out with us, remember? Your Christian friends.

JOY
It's my life. Why can't everyone just leave me alone? Why can't I believe what I want to believe or stop believing in something that I just don't?

HOLLY
What? Joy, listen to you. You're not making any sense.

JOY
(Yelling)
I don't believe any more!

JOY (CONT'D)
(Calming down)
Don't you understand? I don't believe in it any more.

SAMANTHA
Because you've been tricked not to believe!

JOY
No. I was tricked *into* believing. And now my eyes are open.

HOLLY
No Joy. No one tricked you into believing. I've known you all my life. Since we were kids and I've never once seen anyone witness to you. You've always believed. And now you're letting the devil tear our friendship apart. Please, don't do this, Joy.

JOY
I don't know…I need time to clear my head. If you were really my friends, you would let me go.

HOLLY
I can't.

JOY
Why?

HOLLY
I'm my sister's keeper.

(The three girls embrace.)

INT. HAND OF HOPE - IMMEDIATELY AFTER.

(Joy decides to go with her friends. They stop by the foster care building to pick up papers for the church. Still sad, Joy walks off to

*be by herself. Ahdi, who has made a complete turn around, comes
over to greet her.)*

AHDI
What's wrong? Why won't you play with the other girls?

JOY
(Turns and looks down)

Ahdi!
(The two girls hug.)

AHDI
Joy, it's good to see you. I really missed you. I have so much to tell
you. I did just like you said. I've been encouraging the kids and
telling them about Jesus and—

JOY
Wait. Wait. Slow down.

AHDI
God is so good. I mean you just don't know —

JOY
Ahdi—

AHDI
Oh, well I guess you do know. You told me about Him—

JOY
Ahdi—

AHDI
But, you would be so proud of me, Joy. I tell everybody about Jesus
and what you told me. That God watches over us and we don't have
to be scared.

JOY

Ahdi! Stop! I have something to tell you. I was wrong, Ahdi, wrong to tell you those things. Wrong to give you false hope. None of the things I told you were true. They were lies, Ahdi. All lies.

AHDI

But, what about the story you told me?

JOY

I'm sorry, Ahdi, but there is no benevolent King, no God that watches over us. And those people in the story, like you and me, we're on our own.

(Ahdi drops her head.)

JOY (CONT'D)

I'm sorry. Someone told me the truth about God. He doesn't exist. And I feel I should pass that truth on to you. It's better that you are disappointed now while you're still young, than to go on believing all this time and be devastated when you're older.

(A tear falls from Ahdi's eye and hits the ground.)

JOY (CONT'D)

I don't know what's going to happen to you in this place. If someone will ever come for you or if you'll ever leave. I don't even know if there's anyone in the world that even cares. Ahdi, you're all alone. *We're* all alone.

(A second tear falls from Ahdi's eye.)

JOY (CONT'D)

But, I think you should know these things so you can prepare yourself. And Ahdi, I know you're crying, but please understand I never meant to hurt you. Ahdi? Ahdi?

(Ahdi raises her head.)

AHDI
I'm not crying for myself.

JOY
Then why are you crying?

AHDI
 I'm crying for you.

(The child's words pierce Joy's heart.)

AHDI (CONT'D)
You told me the truth about God and I believed you.

JOY
Yes, but it was a lie.

AHDI
Was it a lie when you told it to me?

JOY.
Yes. I mean no—

AHDI
Then why is it a lie now? You're right, Joy. I may never leave this place. But you told me the truth about God when you first came here. I *am* a flower; and we flowers have no control over where God plants us.

(Ahdi opens Joy's hand and places a flower in her palm.)

JOY
What's this?

AHDI
I'm returning a favor. I know you didn't mean to hurt me. I've weighed my options, and I think I'll stay with God.

(Ahdi waves goodbye and runs off to play with the other children. The director walks over to Joy.)

DIRECTOR
Whatever you said to her the last time you were here really affected her. She's a different child now. She runs around encouraging the other children with this amazing story about a king who loves them and looks after little children. You see that child over there?

(The director points to a little girl laughing and playing.)

JOY
Yes.

DIRECTOR
Her name is Cailyn. She was abandoned by her mother, left for dead in one of those drug houses. When the police found her she was barely alive. She hadn't eaten in days. For two weeks she suffered with nightmares, and in the day she would sit in the corner and cry, every so often asking for her mother.

JOY
But she looks fine.

DIRECTOR
I know. You couldn't tell from looking at her that she was traumatized.

JOY
What happened?

DIRECTOR
She met Adhi. That girl is something else. Do you know what Ahdi said to her?

JOY
No.

DIRECTOR
She told her in life . . .

(Joy whispers the words to herself.)

JOY AND DIRECTOR
. . . you can either be someone who is sad or you can be a flower.

(The director turns to face Joy.)

DIRECTOR
…Which one are you?

(Joy looks at the flower in her hand.)

JOY
I thought I was a flower, but now I'm just sad.

(A tear falls from Joy's eye and joins with Ahdi's on the ground. The flower in Joy's hand also hits the ground.)

INT. THE LIVING ROOM OF JOY'S HOUSE - LATER THAT EVENING.

(Joy enters the house to find her father asleep in the chair. In his arms is the photo album open to a picture of Joy laughing as he lifts her into the air. Joy walks over to her father, looks at the photograph, and kisses her father on the forehead. She then takes the photo album and goes upstairs.)

EXT. SCHOOL CAMPUS. - NEXT DAY

(Joy sits at a campus table flipping through the pages of her family Photo album. She is noticeably sick and grabs her chest as her heart begins to race. She reaches into her bag for her medication and notices her cross. After taking her pills, she retrieves her cross and squeezes it tight in her hand. Professor Byrnes comes over to join her.)

PROFESSOR BYRNES
Hi Joy.

JOY
Hi, Professor.

(Joy notices the professor is no longer wearing a bandage on his hand.)

JOY
How's your hand? It's all better now.

PROFESSOR BYRNES
(looking at his hand)
Yes it is. It seems my wounds have been healed.

(Joy closes the photo album and places her philosophy book on top of it.)

PROFESSOR BYRNES
What are you doing?

JOY
Nothing, I was just sitting here thinking.

PROFESSOR BYRNES
Are you all right, Joy? You don't look well.

JOY
I feel a little sick, but I'm okay.

PROFESSOR BYRNES
Are you sure?

JOY
Yes.

PROFESSOR BYRNES
Have you heard about Frankie? He's been expelled.

JOY
Yes, I heard.

PROFESSOR BYRNES
He also confessed to the bomb scare at the abortion clinic a few weeks back. But enough about him, what were you thinking about?

JOY
Life, death, family. I was thinking, Professor, if God does not exist, then what is the purpose of life?

PROFESSOR BYRNES
I'm not sure I'm following you, Joy.

JOY
You know, like family. I mean my relationship with my family is a mess. I've never seen my mother cry as much as she has these past few months, and yet, if there's no God, Professor, what does it matter?

(Joy's eyes close as she speaks.)

PROFESSOR BYRNES
Are you sure you are okay, Joy? I'm worried about you. You don't look well.

JOY
I'm fine; enough about me. We always talk about me, and I don't know much about you.

PROFESSOR BYRNES
That's because you are far more interesting a subject than I could ever be.

JOY
I'm serious, Professor. What do you think about life? About dying? About family?

(Joy opens the photo album and slides it across the table in front of Professor Byrnes.)

PROFESSOR BYRNES
I think families are good for those who are in them.

JOY
You're not answering my question.

PROFESSOR BYRNES
Remember what I taught you. To get the answer you are looking for you have to ask the right question.

JOY
All right, what happened with *your* family, your wife and your daughter? You never told me the story.

PROFESSOR BYRNES
(Looking down at the album)
It's been years since I've been able to look at another family. It was always too painful; but not anymore.

JOY
C'mon Professor.

PROFESSOR BYRNES
I owe you that much.

(Professor Byrnes smiles as he runs his hand across the picture of Mr. Hunter lifting Joy into the air.)

PROFESSOR BYRNES (CONT'D)
I guess every Father does this with his child. As you know, I had a family once; but what you didn't know is that I too once believed.

(Joy's eyes grow heavy as she tries to stay conscious.)

CAMERA SHOT:
MEMORIES OF PROFESSOR BYRNES' DAUGHTER FLASH AS THE CAMERA CIRCLES AROUND JOY AND THE PROFESSOR.

(The narrator begins to speak.)

PROFESSOR BYRNES (NARRATOR)
There is a dynamic that exists between a child and a parent that is beyond words but not expression. An almost spiritual connection in which the *parent's* well being depends on knowing their child is safe. And the thoughts we have of our loved ones, is the mind's way of compensating the heart when they are not in our presence. We think of them, and *we* feel safe. But when they are taken from us, without justification, then the thoughts become memories; and the memories become too painful to bear.

PROFESSOR BYRNES
(Speaking to Joy)
She was the prettiest thing the world had ever seen and when she died, something in me died too, and my marriage just fell apart. The last thing I remember is reading the Bible to her, in her room, and she looked up at me and said, "Daddy help," and then she died.

(Joy's eyes close and she passes out.)

EXT. SCHOOL CAMPUS. – DAY MOMENTS LATER
(Joy opens her eyes and is staring strait up at heaven. She is unaware of what has happened but can feel herself moving. She panics and begins to scream.)

JOY
Nooo! What's happening to me? I don't want to die!

EMT 1
You've got to calm down, otherwise we're gonna have to restrain you further.

JOY
Please, someone, help me! Help meee!

(The EMTs begin to strap Joy down.)

JOY (CONT'D)
No, no, don't do this. Where are you? Father, please help me!

EMT 2
Calm down, honey. We called your parents. They'll be at the hospital to see you. Just relax.

JOY
(Fighting franticly)
No! I don't want to see my family! Not like this!

EMT 1
Her pressure's through the roof.

JOY
Professor, where are you?

PROFESSOR
Yes, Joy. I'm here. Don't worry I'll stay with you. Just let the attendants do their job.

(Joy is rushed away from the place where she had met with Professor Byrnes for the last few months. Both their philosophy of religion books are left behind on the table.)

INT. HOSPITAL. – LATER THAT AFTERNOON

(Professor Byrnes sits in the hospital lounge, waiting for news of Joy.)

NURSE 1
Excuse me. Professor Byrnes?

PROFESSOR
Yes!

NURSE 1
Joy is asking for you. Please come this way.

(As Professor Byrnes enters Joy's room, her Parents come off the elevator and approach one of the nurses on the floor.)

MRS. HUNTER
Where is she? Where's my daughter?

NURSE 2
Mr. & Mrs. Hunter, You can't go in there right now.

MRS. HUNTER
Why not? What's wrong? Oh God, no!

NURSE 2
It's not that, Mrs. Hunter. It's just that she has left specific instructions. She does not want to see you.

MR. HUNTER
She doesn't want to see us?

MRS. HUNTER
Specific instructions? How can she leave instructions? She's seventeen.

MR. HUNTER
Look, get out of my way, that's my daughter in there and I plan to see her.

(The doctor comes over.)

DOCTOR FOSTER
Mr. Hunter, please. Joy was very frantic when they brought her in. We're doing our best to stabilize her, but we need her calm. And if you go in there now, she'll just start right back up again. A Professor Byrnes is in there with her, and he seems to have settled her down.

MR. HUNTER
Professor Byrnes?

DOCTOR FOSTER
I know you want to see your daughter but please, for her sake, give her some time.

(Joy's parents wait down the hall as the doctor speaks to the nurse about Joy.)

DOCTOR FOSTER
(looking at Joy's parents)
It's a shame.

NURSE
What's that, Doctor?

DOCTOR FOSTER
I've been that young girl's physician for the better part of her life, and she has had a wonderful relationship with her family and church. But now she wants nothing to do with them; her family or her God.

NURSE
I never knew you were a religious man, Doctor.

DOCTOR FOSTER
Not particularly. But I must admit, I did enjoy being her doctor. She had such a love for life. Despite her sickness, she had a way of... I don't know, it's just a shame.

NURSE
Something must have happened with her parents.

DOCTOR FOSTER
(looking at Joy's parents)
I don't think it's their fault.

(The doctor then turns and looks at Professor Byrnes as he comes from Joy's room.)

DOCTOR FOSTER (CONT'D)
Somehow I feel he's to blame.

(The Hunters walk over to meet Professor Byrnes)

PROFESSOR BYRNES
Hello, Mr. & Mrs. Hunter?

MRS. HUNTER
Yes.

PROFESSOR BYRNES
I'm Jim Byrnes. Joy's professor.

MR. HUNTER
Yes, we know. We've heard a lot about you.

PROFESSOR BYRNES
Not all bad, I hope.

MR. HUNTER
In fact, it is.

(The professor is shocked at Mr. Hunter's response.)

PROFESSOR BYRNES
Anyway, you are probably curious as to what happened to your daughter. We were sitting on campus talking when she fainted.

MR. HUNTER
You were sitting on campus talking with my daughter!? About what!?

PROFESSOR BYRNES
Excuse me? In any case, the doctors say that your daughter has—

MRS. HUNTER
Mr. Byrnes, she's been our daughter for seventeen years. We know what Joy's condition is.

PROFESSOR BYRNES
Mr. & Mrs. Hunter, maybe I missed something, but I don't understand why you're mad.

MRS. HUNTER
You don't know why we're mad? Have you no respect for the things of God, Mr. Byrnes? The Bible says—

PROFESSOR BYRNES
Oh no! I don't have to stand here and listen to this religious mishmash.

(The professor begins to walk off but Joy's mother stops him.)

MRS. HUNTER
Stop! No you don't! For three months my daughter sat in your class, and for three hours a week listened to your ungodly mishmash. And since I'm her parent, I think you have a responsibility for three minutes to listen to mine!

(Professor Byrnes stops to listen to Mrs. Hunter.)

MRS. HUNTER (CONT'D)
Look at her! Look at her!

(The professor turns and looks at Joy through the window.)

MRS. HUNTER (CONT'D)
For nine months I carried that child. Nine months. I loved her unconditionally before she was born. Even before she had the awareness to know I exist, I loved her. And in three months, three hours a week, you have destroyed all of that. For five years straight, after she was born, she was sick, constantly. *I* prayed with her in the day as she suffered. *I* carried her back and forth to the hospital, slept in that room with her. Me, her mother. I watched with her all night when she was afraid to go to sleep. And in three months, three hours a week, you have destroyed all that. For seventeen years we went to church as a family, prayed, worshiped, laughed, and cried. And in three months, you have destroyed all of that. We have

been close for seventeen years, and now at the end of her life, I can't even go in there and see her! You took my daughter from me and the sad thing is that you don't even realize it. We taught her to trust God, and as a teacher, you destroyed that too. You had a responsibility—

PROFESSOR BYRNES
Don't speak to me about responsibility!

MR. HUNTER
What?! You better stay away from my daughter and stop filling her head with all that atheist crap.

PROFESSOR BYRNES
Mr. Hunter, I teach a class in which your daughter is a student. She is not a child any more. She's in college, and she is mature enough to make her own decision about the course material.

MR. HUNTER
Yes, but if you were a real teacher, you'd realize that you have a responsibility to nurture our children who we've entrusted to your care, not destroy what we taught them about God at home.

PROFESSOR BYRNES
And if your God were real, Mrs. Hunter, he has an even greater responsibility. To be in that room saving that little girl, Faith!

(Mr. Hunter grabs Professor Byrnes.)

MR. HUNTER
Her name is Joy!

(Professor Byrnes realizes that he has made a grave mistake.)

MR. HUNTER (CONT'D)
And if you come near my daughter again, you'll be sorry!

PROFESSOR BYRNES
That's just the kind of response I would expect from a Christian.

(The professor pulls away from Mr. Hunter and walks off. Once out of sight, he retreats into a corner and strikes the wall.)

INT. HOSPITAL. PHONE - IMMEDIATELY AFTER

(Mr. Hunter is on the phone. After he's finished, he hangs up and walks over to his wife, who is talking to the nurse.)

MR. HUNTER
Pastor Rogers is on his way. And he's calling a prayer vigil for her at the church. You better go home and get some rest. I'll wait with her.

MRS. HUNTER
I'm not leaving.

MR. HUNTER
Mel, you should go home and get some rest. Besides the doctor said we can't wait in her room.

NURSE 2
He's right, Mrs. Hunter. You should get some rest.

MRS. HUNTER
I'm not leaving! If I can't stay with her in her hospital room, then I will pray for her in the upper room. Where's the chapel?

NURSE 2
On the first floor, Mrs. Hunter. I'll take you there.

(Joy's parents enter the small chapel. They each take a seat on one of the pews and begin to pray. As they do, the narrator begins to speak.)

PROFESSOR BYRNES (NARRATOR)
Faith, it's a funny thing. It escapes the rational mind's attempt to understand it. It seems mysterious, at times, illogical. Yet the vast majority of humankind is driven to their knees in prayer. Driven to

believe in something. Faith. Huh. It seems so mysterious, so illogical.

INT. TEACHERS LOUNGE - THE FOLLOWING DAY

(Professor Byrnes sits in the teacher's lounge thinking about Mrs. Hunter's words. His mind drifts back to the day he buried his daughter.)

PROFESSOR BYRNES FLASH BACK:
EXT. CEMETERY-DAY

(Scores of people are gathered behind Professor Byrnes and his wife. The Priest begins to speak, as their daughter's small casket is lowered into the ground.)

PRIEST
The Lord giveth and the Lord taketh away . . .

(Upon hearing the priest's words, Professor Byrnes looks angrily toward heaven then turns and walks way.)

CUT TO:

BACK IN TEACHER'S LOUNGE

PROFESSOR BYRNES
You took my daughter.

(Professor Hank walks into the lounge.)

PROF. HANK
So, how is she doing?

PROFESSOR BYRNES
I don't know. She's in the hospital, and her parents have accused me of stealing their daughter because she won't see them or her pastor. The only one she wants to see is me. Is that wrong? All I did was teach a class. She and I eventually became close. I mean, she really is a special girl.

PROF. HANK
Yes, but she's *their* special girl, not yours. Jim, I've been your friend for a long time and though we haven't always agreed, I've never lied to you. You've got to let her go.

PROFESSOR BYRNES
Who? Joy?

PROF. HANK
No, Faith.

PROFESSOR BYRNES
What are you talking about?

PROF. HANK
Joy's not Faith, Jim. She's not your daughter.

(The professor kicks over a magazine stand.)

PROFESSOR BYRNES
I know that damn it! My daughter is dead! Don't you think I know that!

PROF. HANK
And God will—

PROFESSOR BYRNES
God will what, Hank? If there is a God, then he was the one who took her from me! He was the one who took away my Faith, my *joy*. He took her from me.

(The words of Joy's mother linger in the professor's head.)

"You took her from me..."

PROFESSOR BYRNES (CONT'D)
You're right. You are my friend. My Christian friend, and that's why we don't agree.

PROF. HANK
If there is a God, then your daughter belonged to him long before she belonged to you.

(Sitting in the corner of the room, Professor Dean leans in out of the shadows.)

PROF. DEAN
So, what trouble has God caused in the world today?

PROF. HANK
Why do you always say that?

PROF. DEAN
Because I know it upsets you.

PROFESSOR BYRNES
One of my students, Joy, is in hospital, and her parents blame me for her abandoning her faith.

PROF. DEAN
And now you are labeled a devil. It is a small price to pay, Jim, for opening the eyes of the innocent.

PROF. HANK
Just like the serpent, aye Dean?

PROF. DEAN
Funny you should say that. The serpent has gotten a lot of bad press behind that story. But that's because of who's telling the tale.

PROF. HANK
First time I ever heard anyone ask for the devil's side of the story.

PROF. DEAN
That's precisely what I mean. That character in the Bible is not unlike other men in history who have sought to define the world through reason instead of through faith. You see him as the great deceiver. Me, I like to think of him as the father of the enlightenment movement.

PROF. HANK
Oh, he's the father of something, all right.

PROF. DEAN
Think about it. The Bible says he offered them knowledge. He asked them a question, which caused them to think. He asked them, did God really say? And when they took of the fruit, their eyes were opened. Is that not what we as educators do here in college? Give our students knowledge? Ask them questions that cause them to think, thereby opening up their eyes. You did that girl a great service and her parents should be grateful. And if the price she had to pay was a little tension in the family or inner conflict, the knowledge that she gained was well worth it.

PROF. HANK
She's in the hospital, for God's sake, Dean! She could be dying!

PROF. DEAN
Is it his fault!? Did his teachings put her there!?

PROF. HANK
No. But it may have stressed her out.

PROF. DEAN
Nonsense, she was probably unstable from the start. Jim, isn't that the girl that ran out your class earlier in the semester? It is obvious she has some issues that she hasn't dealt with. Besides, how can college prepare her for the world if she can't even stand up to a little controversial discussion in class?

PROF. HANK
College is not supposed to prepare students for the world, their parents are. Our job is to teach them what they have signed up for. Nothing more!

PROF. DEAN
I have two earned Doctorate degrees in the respective fields of history and philosophy. Who knows more about the world, me or them? Or better yet, if their parents know so much, or even cared,

then why do they send their children to college as blank slates for me to teach? If that girl lost her faith, Jim, it's not your fault, it's her parents'. They didn't do a good enough job in that area before she got here. When they come to my class, they don't have to give up their religion if they don't want to. I just present to them the fruit of alternative truth. But it's up to them if they want to take thereof and eat it. No one is forcing them. They are free moral agents. Is that not how your God created them? I just show them what your God does not want them to know.

PROF. HANK
You're being a sarcastic devil.

PROF. DEAN
Purposely. See, unlike you, Hank, and even you, Jim, I look forward to having students like that in my class. Because I govern myself by a higher power, one that is above emotions and religion, one that even science must subject itself to, if even *it* wants to exist.

PROF. HANK
And what is that?

PROF. DEAN
Logic.

(Professor Byrnes looks up at Dean.)

PROF. DEAN (CONT'D)
Things must make sense to the human mind. Why do you think you are in this tumultuous state, Jim? Because you are struggling to make sense of it and the foundation of sensibility is logic. Jim, if you dealt logically with the girl in your class, then your conscience is clear, regardless of what happens to her.

PROF. HANK
God gave us feelings, Dean, another human capacity, so we would have compassion when dealing with one another.

PROFESSOR BYRNES
I had her in my class for three months. Why didn't I notice?

PROF. DEAN
The college classroom is a wonderful place, Professors, where our minds meet, not our hearts. I teach sometimes three classes a day, thirty to forty students per class. You cannot *notice* them all. Nor can you develop feelings for them.

PROF. HANK
No one said it was an easy job, Dean, but as educators we must have compassion.

PROF. DEAN
We don't teach, sir, out of compassion!

PROF. HANK
No! We don't! But God and their parents expect that we will.

(For seconds, the two professors stare at each other. Then Prof. Dean smirks.)

PROF. DEAN
Well, I am not employed by their parents...
(Professor Dean slumps in his chair, and back into the shadows.)

PROF. DEAN (CONT'D)
—nor do I serve your God.

INT. HOSPITAL. - EVENING

(The nurse walks in to see about Joy.)

NURSE
Good evening Joy. How are you feeling?

JOY
I feel weak and very tired. Do you know where my things are?

NURSE
All your clothes are in the closet.

JOY
No. Not those. I had a photo album, but I don't see it among my things.

NURSE
(Fixing Joy's bed)
What's in that closet and in that bag are all that the EMT brought in when you arrived. I don't remember seeing a photo album.

(Joy turns toward the window and Pastor Rogers walks in.)

PASTOR ROGERS
Hey, Joy. How are you doing, child?

(Joy does not respond.)

PASTOR ROGERS (CONT'D)
We've missed you in church, so I came out to see you, and I bring the love and prayers of all the saints. Everyone's been asking about you.

JOY
Don't you mean talking about me?

PASTOR ROGERS
No, dear. The church is not like that. Everyone goes through hard times. Your church family understands. Besides half the people in there, you helped win to Christ.

JOY
Pastor? Do you know what's going to happen to me?

PASTOR ROGERS
Yes, Joy. The doctors have told me.

JOY
That's not what I mean. I'm afraid.

PASTOR ROGERS
I know.

JOY
But that's just it. I *don't* know what's going to happen to me. Not anymore. Why couldn't this happen to me two years ago, when they said it would.

PASTOR ROGERS
Don't say that Joy.

JOY
I was ready then.

PASTOR ROGERS
I know what the doctors told your parents when you were born, but obviously that wasn't God's will. You're here because He has something greater for you to do.

JOY
What, for me to question him?

PASTOR ROGERS
Only He knows why He extended your life; but even though you don't see Him, God's here. He loves you and He knows the way that you take.

JOY
No Pastor. I'm not wor—

(Joy turns away.)

PASTOR ROGERS
You're not what?

(Pastor Rogers waits for a reply but Joy suddenly turns on him.)

JOY (CONT'D)
Pastor, you've got to leave!

PASTOR ROGERS
Joy, I just want to pray for you.

JOY
No prayer. You can't help me this time. I want you to leave. Right
now!

PASTOR ROGERS
Joy, I don't understand.

JOY
Just leave! Nurse! Nurse!

(The nurses rush in to the room.)

PASTOR ROGERS
Joy, please!

JOY
Leave! Leave! I want you to leave!

(The nurses usher the pastor from the room.)

NURSE
You have to leave, Pastor. You are upsetting the patient.

PASTOR ROGERS
I just want to help. I just want to—

*(As the nurses pull Pastor Rogers into the hallway, he realizes what
Joy was trying to say.)*

PASTOR ROGERS
"Worthy"

(The Pastor tries to re-enter the room but is stopped by the nurses. He makes eye contact with Joy and she turns away.)

INT. HOSPITAL LOBBY. – LATER THAT EVENING

(Holly and Samantha come to visit Joy. They speak to the receptionist to find her room.)

SAMANTHA
Hi. We're here to see Joy Hunter.

HOSPITAL RECEPTIONIST
One moment. Oh, yes. She is in room 314, but she is not receiving visitors.

HOLLY
Oh, she'll receive us. Where are the elevators?

HOSPITAL RECEPTIONIST
Young lady, I said she is not receiving visitors. The hospital rules are there for a reason. Your friend may be very sick or even under sedation. And if that were the case, she wouldn't even know you were there.

SAMANTHA
Thank you, ma'am.

(Samantha pulls Holly away from the desk.)

SAMANTHA (CONT'D)
What's wrong with you? Since when is disrespect one of the fruits of the spirit?

HOLLY
I'm not leaving here till I see my sister.

SAMANTHA
You heard what she said. What are we going to do?

HOLLY
Follow me.

SAMANTHA
All right, but can you at least try to act like a Christian?

(The girls take the elevator to the third floor. They begin looking for room 314 and are stopped by a nurse.)

NURSE
Excuse me, ladies. May I help you?

HOLLY
Ah. Yes. We are here to visit someone.

NURSE
Who are you here to see? What room are they in?

HOLLY
Room? Uh, they're in room—

SAMANTHA
316. We're looking for John. Uhh …316.

NURSE
Oh. I don't know about John, but room 316 is down the hall to the right.

SAMANTHA AND HOLLY
Thank you.

HOLLY
"John 316?"

SAMANTHA
Don't look at me like that. I thought she was asking for my favorite scripture.

(The two girls enter the room and find their friend fast asleep. One walks to the foot of the bed; the other takes her place by Joy's side and they each begin to pray. After pulling the covers over Joy's shoulders, they leave the picture they took at graduation by her bed and exit the room.)

CUT TO:
JOY'S CHURCH

(A young girl walks into Joy's church and is noticed by one of the women ushers. She is wearing jeans, a sweater, and a black pea coat. Her face is covered by a hooded scarf)

USHER
Hello. May I help you?

GIRL
I was walking by and I saw the church was open. I'm looking for Pastor Rogers. A friend told me when I made my decision, he would pray with me. And I've made my decision.

USHER
And what decision is that?

(The young girl removes the hooded scarf from her face.)

DEBBIE
I'm no longer uncertain. I believe in God.

(The usher leads Debbie to the empty prayer chapel in the church.)

USHER
Pastor Rogers is not here, but one of the elders can pray with you.

DEBBIE
If it's not a problem?

USHER
Not at all; but I'm curious. What did your friend say to you that
changed your mind?

DEBBIE
She lead me out the back door of an abortion clinic and she told
me, when my baby was born, to set things right. She told me to
look her in the eyes and tell her,

*"You don't have to die, so I can live my life; but I promise you, I
will give my life so that you can live yours."*

And then she said, that's what Jesus did for me.

USHER
Tell me dear, who is your friend?

DEBBIE
Joy. Joy Hunter.

USHER
Oh. You know your friend is not here.

DEBBIE
Yes. She said she wouldn't be coming back.

USHER
No, I mean she's in the hospital. Pastor Rogers went earlier to see
her.

DEBBIE
Then why's the chapel empty? This is her church, why isn't anyone
praying for her?

USHER
Come with me.

(The usher leads Debbie to the doors of the main sanctuary.)

USHER (CONT'D)
When we found out about Joy, the pastor called a vigil. The chapel could not accommodate all those who came to pray for her.

(The usher opens the doors to the main sanctuary to reveal a sea of people, all praying for Joy. Down in front are Richard and Kevin who is staring at one of the Bibles in the back of the pews.)

USHER (CONT'D)
Pastor said despite her present condition, he feels God has one more task for her to complete.

INT. PROFESSOR BYRNES HOUSE - EVENING

(The drawer in the professor's bedroom is open and the photographs that were locked inside are scattered all over the floor. The trail of broken pictures leads down the hall to his daughter's room where the professor stands in the door way, holding a Bible in his bleeding hand.)

(The phone rings)

PROFESSOR BYRNES
Hello?

DOCTOR FOSTER
Yes, this is Dr. Foster from the hospital. Are you Professor Byrnes?

PROFESSOR BYRNES
Yes, I am.

DOCTOR FOSTER
Miss Hunter has taken a turn for the worst and she's asking for you.

PROFESSOR BYRNES
For me, aren't her parents there?

DOCTOR FOSTER
Yes. They're here, but she won't see them. You are the only one she wants to see.

PROFESSOR BYRNES
I understand. I'll be right there.

(Professor Byrnes repeatedly slams the receiver against the wall.)

PROFESSOR BYRNES (CONT'D)
It's happening again. She's dying and there's nothing I can do to help her. I can't watch her die again.

(Looking up to heaven)

Please . . . if you're real . . . help her.

INT. HOSPITAL – IMMEDIATELY AFTER

(Professor Byrnes stands outside of Joy's room staring at his bandaged hand and trying to muster the courage to see Joy. The doctor walks out of the room after checking Joy's vitals. The professor stops him and inquires about her condition.)

PROFESSOR BYRNES
Doctor, may I speak to you for a minute?

DOCTOR FOSTER
Yes. What's on your mind, Mr. Byrnes?

PROFESSOR BYRNES
She's dying, isn't she?

DOCTOR FOSTER
Her vitals are dropping.

PROFESSOR BYRNES
Is she dying?

DOCTOR FOSTER
Yes, but she shouldn't be.

PROFESSOR BYRNES
What!?

DOCTOR FOSTER
It's a bit complicated. Joy does have a rare condition. In the past, we've been able to control it. But this time, something's different. I assure you though; we're doing everything medically possible to help her.

PROFESSOR BYRNES
I don't understand. If it's treatable, you give her the medication and she gets better…

(The professor grabs the doctor's arm.)

PROFESSOR BYRNES (CONT'D)
If she's still dying, then there's something you're doing wrong!

DOCTOR FOSTER
Mr. Byrnes, you may be a history teacher, but medicine and biology are my areas of expertise, and here is a revelation for you.

(The doctor removes the professor's hand from his arm.)

DOCTOR FOSTER (CONT'D)
There is more to this world than what we can see with our eyes or ever understand with our tiny little brains, and that's coming from a medical doctor.

PROFESSOR BYRNES
You're a physician, and she's dying, doctor! It's your job to not let that happen!

DOCTOR FOSTER
Mr. Byrnes, she's not dying because her body's sick. She's dying because her soul is sick!

PROFESSOR BYRNES
What?

DOCTOR FOSTER
She's not fighting anymore. She's lost the will to live. Her depression is causing other complications, and her body, which is already sick, is responding in kind! You're the skeptic; how do we treat that?

(The doctor walks off and the professor strikes the wall by Joy's room. Joy now knows someone is there.)

JOY
Professor?

PROFESSOR BYRNES
Yes, Joy. I'm here.

(Professor Byrnes walks into the room and sees Joy hooked up to monitors and tubes.)

PROFESSOR BYRNES
They said you were asking for me.

JOY
You hurt your hand again?

PROFESSOR BYNES
Yes. It seems we've both had a relapse.

JOY
Professor, what do you think is going to happen to me?

PROFESSOR BYRNES
Well, the doctor said—

JOY
No. That's not what I mean. What will happen to me when I die?

PROFESSOR BYRNES
I... Ah... the body...when the brain looses consciousness— Ah

JOY
Where will I go?

PROFESSOR BYRNES
You don't . . . actually . . . I don't know. Listen, enough with that. Joy, the doctor told me something that doesn't make sense. He said you should be getting better. But you're not. It's as if you want to die.

(Joy turns her head away.)

PROFESSOR BYRNES (CONT'D)
Joy, talk to me.

JOY
Professor, do you know how I feel?

PROFESSOR BYRNES
No.

JOY
Alone, I feel alone. I miss my mom, my dad, my friends and Professor...

PROFESSOR BYRNES
Yes?

JOY
I miss my God. But I feel like I let him down, like I have abandoned Him. I don't want to die.

PROFESSOR BYRNES
Then you've got to fight, Joy. Fight to live!

JOY
You don't understand. More than I don't want to die . . . I don't want to live.

PROFESSOR BYRNES
Why not?

JOY
You've made me think about a lot of things since I've been in your class. If God doesn't exist, then why should I fight? What does it matter? Evil, whether you kill, whether you hate. What does it matter, if there's no God?

(Joy looks toward heaven.)

JOY (CONT'D)
Then I might as well die. And if He does exist—

PROFESSOR BYRNES
The question of suffering?

JOY
No. I don't care about my suffering anymore. If he exists, then I've let him down. And I can't live with that.

JOY (CONT'D)
I feel afraid, scared, like I did when I was little. That's why I called you, Professor.

PROFESSOR BYRNES
Tell me, how can I help?

JOY
I feel like I'm up on a ledge, and there's no one to talk me down.

PROFESSOR BYRNES
Joy, no. Don't do this to me.

JOY
I don't know if He still loves me, I don't know if He exists.

PROFESSOR BYRNES
You should really be talking to your parents.

JOY
No. My parents aren't supposed to be here right now. I called for you. Please, Professor. You've always had the answers. I feel my soul slipping away and I need something to hold on to.

(Joy reaches out to the professor but he pulls his bandaged hand away.)

PROFESSOR BYRNES
I . . . can't. I don't . . . have . . . the answer.

(Joy turns her head to the wall, and begins to cry.)

PROFESSOR BYRNES (CONT'D)
Help me.

(His own eyes fill with tears and he turns his head toward heaven.)

PROFESSOR BYRNES (CONT'D)
Please God . . . Help her. Let her live. Give me something to say.

(Suddenly, Paul's words enter the professor's mind.)

"Things are not eternal because men discovered them to be. Things are eternal—"

PROFESSOR BYRNES
(Speaking to himself)
—because God has made them so.

(A look of awe slowly crosses the professor's face.)

"You would not have believed the universe to be eternal if someone you trusted had not told you so. Yet the universe is eternal whether you believe it or not. Likewise it is with the human soul."

PROFESSOR BYRNES
I believe.

"Then trust me ..."

(Professor Byrnes falls to his knees.)

"You will see your daughter again."

(He can no longer hold back the tears.)

PROFESSOR BYRNES
Forgive me God.

JOY
Professor?

PROFESSOR BYRNES
Yes, Joy.

JOY
I never read the book you gave me.

(The professor looks up and smiles.)

JOY (CONT'D)
Are you mad?

PROFESSOR BYRNES
No, Joy. I am actually glad you never read that stupid book. And as a teacher I have to apologize to you.

JOY
For what?

PROFESSOR BYRNES
For telling you how to think based on *my* experience with God and because there was a book that *I* should have read and never did.

JOY
(speaking faintly)
What's that?

PROFESSOR BYRNES
Your life.

JOY
(crying)
No, professor, I've made a mess of my life; my parents and my God. I left Him.

(Professor Byrnes sees the alabaster cross tightly held in Joy's hand)

PROFESSOR BYRNES
(Opening Joy's hand)
Look. You haven't left Him, Joy. You've held on to Him all this time. And because of you, I now know that He never left me.

JOY
Professor, I'm sorry. I *tried* not to, but I *still* believe in God.

PROFESSOR BYRNES
I know. So do I.

(Professor Byrnes reaches over and embraces Joy.)

PROFESSOR BYRNES
You're hot, and your heart is racing.

(He reaches for the distress button by her bed to call for the nurse but Joy grabs his hand.)

JOY
Professor, I'm not afraid anymore.

(The professor sobs uncontrollably.)

JOY (CONT'D)
I'll see you again.
(A peaceful smile crosses Joy's face. As her arms drops to the bed side, the cross she was holding falls out her hand and she dies. Joy's parents rush into the room. Her father throws the professor to the side and Professor Byrnes' eyes fix on the crucifix lying on the ground.)

FADE TO BLACK

BACK TO THE OPENING SCENE.

(The professor sits at his desk looking at Joy's photo album. Before leaving for the funeral, he finishes his reflections.)

PROFESSOR BYRNES (NARRATOR)
So, what is the relationship between a student and a teacher? It is just that, a relationship. A teacher must teach the assigned subject and the student must learn the assigned subject without the crossing of professional boundaries or the abuse of personal rights. Such rights as respect, trust and yes, even the right to believe. As an educator, my job was to teach her. Not to influence her against God. But, who would have thought that God would have used her to influence me?

(The professor opens his hand. Sitting in his palm is Joy's alabaster cross, the edges having been worn down.)

PROFESSOR BYRNES (NARRATOR)
Faith. It's a funny thing—

SCENE MONTAGE:

CUT TO: DEBBIE'S APT

(Debbie is in the room reading the Bible to her little girl playing in her crib.)

PROFESSOR BYRNES (NARRATOR)
It escapes the rational mind's attempt to understand it.

CUT TO:
KEVIN'S PARENT'S HOME

(Kevin knocks on the door of his parent's house. He is dressed in a pair of black converse sneakers, jeans, and plain white tee shirt. A watch replaces the lace glove that covered his wrist.)

PROFESSOR BYRNES (NARRATOR)
It seems mysterious—

(Kevin's mother opens the door and embraces her son.)

PROFESSOR BYRNES (NARRATOR)
At times illogical.

(Kevin sits in the living room with his parents and shows them a Bible. The inscription reads, "The Oil of Joy")

PROFESSOR BYRNES (NARRATOR)
Yet, ironically, the foundation of faith is logic.

CUT TO:
JOY'S CHURCH

(The youth of the church are gathered in the teaching hall and Pastor Rogers is lecturing.)

PROFESSOR BYRNES (NARRATOR)
Every effect has a cause...

(Behind him on a large flat screen monitor is the subject being taught. It reads, "Christian World views vs. Secular World Views. Defending what you believe.")

PROFESSOR BYRNES (NARRATOR)
Just like a ripple.

CUT TO:
THE HANDS OF HOPE ORPHANAGE

(A young couple has come to give Ahdi a home.)

PROFESSOR BYRNES (NARRATOR)
And as long as I am aware of the ripples…the effects…

(Ahdi walks over to Cailyn, and gives her a hand full of flowers. The two girls embrace and say their goodbyes.)

PROFESSOR BYRNES (NARRATOR)
Then logic demands that I believe in some form of cause.

(Ahdi turns and runs into the arms of her new parents and gives them a hug.)

PROFESSOR BYRNES (NARRATOR)
Even if I can't see it.

CUT TO:
PRESENT DAY - JOY'S BURIAL

(Scores of people holding flowers have gathered to mourn the loss of their beloved Joy. Among them are Debbie, Mrs. Byrnes, and others who Joy's life has touched. Professor Byrnes stares at Joy's casket which is covered in flowers and a small sign which reads—)

"Unless a seed is planted in the earth and dies, it remains alone. But in its death it will produce a rich harvest of new lives. John 12:24"
(Professor Byrnes holds onto Joy's mother as the casket is lowered into the ground.)

PROFESSOR BYRNES (NARRATOR)
Faith. How could I have missed it? It's the substance of things hoped for, the evidence of things not seen. And each individual, whether student or teacher, has the right to believe.

(Professor Byrnes looks at Pastor Rogers, then up at God, and smiles.)

****

END

EPILOGUE

Reviving of the Vision

Jessica walked out the door of the college gymnasium and into the campus parking lot. She flung her gym bag over her shoulder and looked across the lot to the other side.

I have five minutes to get to the bus stop, she thought.

Any other time during the day the lot would be full, but at this late hour only five cars stood between her and the exit. Jessica looked up the street to her left. On the other side of the gate she could see the big lights of the bus coming from a few blocks away, but just in front of the exit was a young lady standing by a car, frantically going through her bag. As Jessica neared the entrance, the face of the worried girl became familiar.

"Katie? Is that you?" Jessica asked.

"Oh! Hi, Jessica," the panicked girl replied, as she continued to search through her bag.

"Is everything Okay?"

"No not really. I-I can't find my keys."

On the other side of the gate, Jessica's bus pulled up and began to take on passengers, but Jessica turned to her friend.

"Girl, you must have a lot on your mind."

"Why would you say that?"

"Because, your keys are right there in your hand!"

Katie dropped her bag and began to cry, holding the keys to her face. Jessica walked over and embraced her friend. On the other side of the gate, the bus closed its doors and pulled away from the curb.

"I'm so embarrassed," Katie said as she dried her tears with the back of her hands. "Please, Jessica, let me give you a ride home."

File
Save

T-h-e- M-i-s-e-d-u-c-a-t-i-o-n- o-f- J-o-y
Enter

There, it was finally done. What seemed to be one long intense day had actually taken Paul nine months to write. That which was downloaded and filled his mind for the better part of a year, was now uploaded onto his word processor. But what was the next move? Paul had asked himself this question halfway through the story, at about page eighty–three, and he had received what he believed was an answer.

> *"Go to the leaders of the church, Godly men who have been entrusted with great resources and have been placed in positions of great influence and power. Go, and tell them the vision."*

The plan had come so instantaneously after he prayed that he felt it had to be inspired by God. On top of that, he knew three friends that would be able to get him an audience with these great leaders. But that was the plan a hundred pages ago. Since then, Paul had done everything that he purposed in his heart to do. He had reached out to his contacts, he had reached out to the leaders on his list; actually speaking to three of them and the initial meeting seemed very promising. He even reached out to Christian film companies; but now, a hundred pages later—nothing. No calls, no meetings, no e-mails. It seemed like everyone had moved on. Whenever Paul turned on the radio or the TV, the men whom he had reached out to were always working on a new project. Ironically, the only people who showed any interest were non- Christian groups. It wasn't that Paul did not want to use secular means to advance his project, but it just seemed more appropriate to him to have the film supported by a faith-based group.

Paul stared at the finished script on his computer screen as if waiting for it to answer.

Why?

He suddenly felt like Joy, the character in his film, but he was not questioning God, he was questioning man.

Why haven't they seen the vision?

He was questioning the system.

Why haven't they supported?

And, he was questioning himself.

What am I doing wrong?

Doubt set in.

Have you ever felt like you did everything God had asked you to do but still no breakthrough? Having a dream and doing your best, but all your efforts ending in disappointment, as if you were destined not to succeed at anything? This is how Paul felt; like he was too small, and his idea too big.

"What's wrong with me?" He said to himself angrily. "I'm not a filmmaker, I'm not an author."

Paul looked around his room at the mounds of research books and video equipment he bought to shoot the trailer for the film.

"I'm just a man who has wasted a lot of time and money on a dream. How could I have been so foolish to think I could complete so great a task?"

"Paul!"

Joanne, Paul's wife, called to him from downstairs, but he did not answer; instead, he stared at the textbook on top of his desk. It read, *Philosophy of Religion*. It was the assigned reader for the latest class he had registered for at college and the professor had arranged a meeting with the department chairman to have Paul removed from the class.

It's an online course. How could I get kicked out of an online course in the first week? Maybe they're right. Secularism is not the problem, I am. I don't even know what really happened to that girl in my history class. Maybe she's fine and doesn't need someone to stand up for her rights—

"Paul!" His wife called again from downstairs. This time he answered, turning his head to the door.

"Yes?"

"It's your sister, Jessica. She's outside in a car with a friend."

"Well, tell her to come in."

"She said no, you have to come out."

Paul looked at the PC monitor. His script faded out of sight as the computer entered sleep mode.

A disappointed grin crossed his face and he shook his head.

"I hear you God," Paul said sadly. "It was just a dream, but I guess life leaves you no time for dreams."

Paul got up and headed downstairs. At the dining room table sat Paul's seven-year-old son, reluctantly doing school work and quick to look up as his father walked by.

"Dad, where are you going? I need you to help me with my homework."

"When I come back, little buddy," Paul answered.

It's time I got back to my own life. I have issues at my church, my school—

"Yes, and dinner's almost ready, so don't think you're going back on that computer, Mr. Agard," called the voice from the kitchen.

Paul stopped and looked at his wife.

"You don't have to worry about that anymore, babe."

Paul opened the front door and the night air hit his face. He felt relieved as if a burden had been lifted from off his shoulders. But somewhere deep inside him, he also felt the tug of failure. He tried to reassure himself.

Just because I have an issue with religious rights in America, doesn't mean everybody else does.

Outside, a black Ford sat parked in front of his house. It wasn't a Mustang, but it was enough to take him back to that inter-section where he hesitated. As he walked to the car, he couldn't help but remember the words of the song.

"You only get one shot."

Now, all Paul felt was failure.

"Talk to me Lord, please."

Jessica got out the car and sat in the back, motioning to her brother to sit in the front seat. Paul walked around the front of the car, but the driver paid no attention to him. Instead, she stared straight ahead, with both hands clutching the steering wheel. Paul opened the passenger side door, got in, and closed it behind him. Inside, he found a distraught twenty-year-old girl carrying a greater burden than his.

"This is my friend, Katie," Jessica said from the back seat. "She's dealing with a spiritual crisis, Paul, and I told her you'd be able to help her."

Wow, that's some tall order. He thought; but he quickly responded to encourage his sister and Katie.

"Well, prayfully the Lord will allow me to do so. How can I help?"

"Katie has been studying European history at my old college, and the professor has been teaching her how *evil* Christians are," Jessica said, leaning forward and placing her hand on Katie's shoulder. "And now she's questioning her faith."

Suddenly, Katie broke her silence.

"We've murdered Jews, Muslims, and unbelievers," she said in a cold and desperate voice, her eyes still staring straight ahead. "If Christians have done so much evil in the world, how could they be right? That's what the instructor said to me. And if *he's* right, then how can I go on being a Christian?"

"That's when I told her about your movie," Jessica quickly interjected. "I told her, my brother Paul can help you."

Katie turned and looked at Paul, who responded with a smile.

Twenty minutes later, Paul exited the black Ford and hurried toward his front door. From behind, a reassured Katie called out to him.

"Thank you Brother Paul, for everything and may God always bless you."

Paul ran in the house and up the stairs.

"Hey! Where do you think you're going?" His wife called as he ran by her. "I'm setting the table for dinner."

"I'll be right back," he replied, as he ran up the stairs.

Paul opened his bedroom door, lunged into his computer chair, and spun it around toward his PC. He tapped the space bar three times and the screen came to life, the script now staring at Paul as if *it* was waiting for an answer.

What are you going to do with me? What are you going to do with me?

"If God gave me this vision, he doesn't want it to stay on my hard drive," he asserted.

Paul's pity party had come to an abrupt end. He was now aware of what had happened earlier. Depression had called him out to the open desert and challenged him to a fight, just like it does every person trying to fulfill their dream, but *only* Paul had returned from the dry sands, leaving depression and self-pity behind.

"Thank you, Lord," he said looking up to heaven. Paul sat back in his chair and recalled Katie's words to him:

"If the professor's right, how can I go on being a Christian?"

A strange but familiar feeling came over Paul. He had felt it almost a year ago, when *his* history professor said that science and faith could not be reconciled, and then pressured that young girl into giving up one. But that happened two hundred pages and fifteen hundred computer hours ago.

"It's still wrong," Paul said to himself. He now felt driven. Driven by God, driven by morality, and sadly, driven by himself. Driven to prove he was not a failure, driven to make his family proud, and driven to finish what he had started for the Lord. At the end of the day, Paul was not an author, he was not a filmmaker, but he was driven. The only thing in life he was ever really good at was *Jesus*, and it was as if God had somehow given this little man a great responsibility. Passages of Scripture now ran through his mind, where just moments ago doubt had settled in.

> *"Write the vision down. It is the answer to an injustice that has long been carried out on all people who choose to believe, as this nation seeks to become more secular. Write the vision down and make it plain . . ."*

"I did that L—"

Before he could finish the sentence, the download began anew.

> *"So he who reads it will run with it. The word will be published. It goes forth and does not return void."*

"That's it!" Paul said out loud. "This is 2009, and there's more than one way to get God's word out."

Paul's fingers moved across the keyboard.

G-o-o-g-l-e

Enter

S-e-l-f – p-u-b-l-i-s-h-i-n-g
Enter
Paul looked at the choices on the screen. One stood out from among the rest.

"www.Dog Ear Publishing.com"
Paul clicked on the site and read the caption out loud.
"Express yourself in print."

"Yes, write the vision down and make it plain, and everyone who reads it will run with it. Everyone who believed in the First Amendment, in religious freedom, everyone who bought the book, and eventually saw the movie, they would be the ones to run with it."

This was not the end of his dream, this was only the beginning. Paul filled out the necessary fields and submitted his manuscript.

"Paul! Dinner's ready!" His wife called out to him from downstairs.

"Okay, I'm coming."

Paul's daughter, Krysten, entered the room.

"Daddy, Mom said it's time to come downstairs." Paul looked into his daughter's eyes and smiled.

"Go 'head, babe," he said. "I'll be there in a minute. I promise."

The only thing left to do was pray. Paul folded his hands, bowed his head in front of the computer, and uttered seven words.

"Father, please. Make this vision a reality."

****

Resources

There were many topics raised by my professors and some classmate that were either intended to discredit my faith or to cause doubt. Over the years, I have had to develop an extensive resource list in which to reference in class discussions and debates. Below is a starter list of some great resources that have helped me move forward in secular colleges with the integrity of my faith leading the way.

Websites
http://www.answersingenesis.org/
http://www.carm.org/
http://www.apologeticspress.org/
http://www.christiananswers.net/
http://www.rose-publishing.com/
http://www.christianbook.com/

Christian leaders
* RC. Sproul - http://www.ligonier.org/
* Hank Hannergraff - http://www.equip.org/
* Lee Strobel - http://www.leestrobel.com/
* Dr. James Dobson - http://www.focusonthefamily.com/
* Chuck Swindol - http://www.insight.org/site/PageServer
.

Books
Icons of Evolution by Johnathan Wells
Evolution: The Grand Experiment by Carl Werner
The Case For Christ by Lee Strobel
The Case For A Creator by Lee Strobel
Rose Book of Bible Charts, Maps, Time Lines, Vol. 1
Evidence that Demands a Verdict by Josh Mcdowell
Church history in Plain Language by Bruce L. Shelly

Video
http://www.thehopeproject.com/
New Evidence that Demands a Verdict DVD video

*From the above list of resources and websites, you will have access to an even greater vault of educational videos, books, and other resources that are too numerous to list here.

*I am currently working on a book that addresses the issues students of faith may face while in college. It is my hope to collaborate with the leaders of our faith to accomplish this task.

LaVergne, TN USA
21 July 2010
190411LV00001B/10/P